PROXYFLANS

The Magical Girl in PROXY

I

I Woke Up One Morning and Discovered I'm a Magical Girl Mascot

PROXYFLANS

The Magical Girl in PROXY:
I Woke Up One Morning and Discovered I'm a Magical Girl Mascot

©2024 PROXYFLANS

PROXYFLANS.com

OFL Fonts Used:
EB Garamond by Georg Duffner
Hina Mincho by satsuyako

ISBN (paperback): 978-1-963350-00-5

ISBN (eBook): 978-1-963350-01-2

For those who woke up one day with a little extra magic in their lives,

And for those who haven't yet felt that spark:

A love letter to magical girls.

They have a job that someone has to do.

EPISODE ONE

NANA DROPLETS

OOI

Doll Park was—in Ueno Suzu's experience—best defined by its food, thrill rides that were barely thrilling, and the cutest plush souvenirs. While Suzu enjoyed the food, she knew her parents could buy something similar for much less at the convenience store. She was also stuck between being too tall for the rides she once enjoyed, and not tall enough for the rides she wanted to try. Finally, while the plushies were well-made, she never kept them past the end of the year because she had a mountain of stuffed animals looming in the corner of her bedroom.

Of course, none of this would stop her from joining her friends when they invited her—especially when their parents were offering to buy the pricey admission tickets. Seeing as she was free after school, it would be rude to decline. And so, Suzu—still in her *seifuku*—found herself following her two classmates and their respective mothers onto the train after school. Unfortunately, her own mother couldn't attend.

And through the park entrance they walked—the atmosphere seeming to change as they exited the blazing sun, into the momentary shade of the overhang, and back into the sun.

The air was fresh, with a slight breeze. The oppressive heat lifted away.

Suzu reached around her neck for her neon green headphones before stopping herself—shutting down her friends and their mothers before someone even initiated any conversation would *also* be rude.

"Sakiko, Moe...th-thank you again for inviting me," she said for the sixth time since getting off the train, nervously poking her index fingers together.

"We love having you with us," Moe replied, shrugging dismissively. She raised her nose to the oncoming breeze, closing her eyes as she gave the air a few quick sniffs. "I think they have *crêpes!*" she shouted over her shoulder as she took off. Her mother quickly followed to ensure she had enough money to pay for one.

Sakiko sighed. "*Moe...*"

Suzu and Sakiko sat on a blue, plastic bench, awaiting the return of their friend.

A rainbow-colored form caught Suzu's attention in the corner of her eye. "Oh, *balloons!*"

"Would you like one?" Sakiko's mother asked, reaching for her purse.

"Yes!" Suzu replied, hopping off the bench. "I-I'll pay for it, though! Don't worry!"

Not wanting to be more of a burden than she felt she already was, Suzu turned back and made her way through the crowd, eyes locked on the balloon cart. It was then that a lovestruck couple bumped into her, and she tumbled to the ground.

She stood up and realized that in the confusion, she had gotten spun around—losing sight not only of the balloon cart, but of Sakiko and her mother.

Suzu started walking in the direction she thought she had come from. She arrived at a blue, plastic bench—though there were lots of blue benches, so she couldn't be sure.

It was unoccupied.

It's okay, she said to herself, putting on her headphones. "I'll find them."

And so, she wandered around the amusement park, looking for her friends and their mothers, or anyone who could assist her in locating them. This was when she noticed two older girls across the plaza from herself—one in a high school uniform, and the other in a prestigious university's uniform.

Suzu decided to approach them, since *something* about them seemed safe—most likely the fact that both of them seemed to be as equally perplexed as she was. Their contrasting uniforms also made them stand out from not only each other, but the other park-goers. She slid her headphones off, shaking out her choppy, purple hair.

"Hi! I...just noticed you both from over t-there. Are...you lost, too?"

The taller of the two girls—the university student—stepped forward, uneasily. Her long, white ponytail slipped off her shoulder, falling down her back. "Yes, I guess we are."

The other girl—who had long, wavy hair the fascinating color of dying embers—opened her mouth to add something.

Crash!

The only noise that came out of her was a small, *Eek!*

An enormous monster resembling a black salamander towered over the park. Parents screamed and ran, dragging or carrying their resisting children who wanted to stay and watch what they mistook for a *very* high-tech hero show.

Suzu caught a glimpse of familiar *seifuku* out of the corner of her eye. "Sakiko!" she screamed, turning in her schoolmates' direction. "Moe!" The monster's roars drowned out her screams.

She would have followed the two girls—regardless of whether or not they were her friends—but found herself frozen in place, holding the two older girls' hands instinctively.

Her nails just about dug into their skin, though they showed no pain.

Suddenly, two strange rabbits materialized in front of the trio of girls—one black with purple eyes, the other mint green with milky eyes. Light matching their respective eye colors engulfed the strange creatures, and they zoomed at the monster, appearing as two vibrant streaks in the air.

"Your enemy is approaching!" the black rabbit shouted in a deep voice—more fitting for a grown man. "Suzu! Noriko! Atsuko! The three of you must take action *now!*"

"*Eh?*" If Suzu's legs weren't shaking before from the sudden appearance of the monster, they definitely were now at the thought of having to become involved. "What do you *mean,* 'enemy'? What *is* that thing? What are *you?* And what do you mean we have to 'take action'?"

The monster's tail demolished a ride—the drop tower—and the wreckage landed close to the trio.

Too close.

A blast of air mussed up the girls' hair, and their clothes rippled about.

"Yeah, can't you get someone else to do it?" Atsuko, the high school student, brushed her hair out of her face. "I was just minding my own business—I don't even *know* these girls."

"*No!*" the green rabbit exclaimed in the shrill voice of a little boy. Suzu then realized the rabbits weren't actually shouting—with all the devastation around them it would be impossible to hear. Instead, the trio could hear their voices telepathically. "The three of you have done this before! You need to *remember!*"

She just told you—Noriko insisted. "The three of us have never met before in our lives!"

There were nods of agreement.

The monster swatted a tree, which crash-landed a few meters from the trio—closer than the ride had fallen.

"I just wanna go *home!*" Suzu shrieked, releasing the girls' hands as she crouched down, pulling her headphones over her ears to drown out the chaos.

The green rabbit emitted a cone of light from his head, directing it at the girls. It got wider and wider, until the girls were standing in what was, from their perspective, a cylinder. Suzu's expression changed to one of confidence as she stood tall.

The girls looked at each other with a sudden sense of recognition before turning to the rabbits.

Yes—they *did* know each other! And they had met the rabbits before—Elves in disguise—under similar circumstances years ago, when monsters had swarmed their city.

Suzu no longer looked at the two girls as strangers, but as her best friends—Takahashi Noriko and Oshiro Atsuko.

"Jet!" Noriko shouted in relieved recognition.

"Bone!" Atsuko happily exclaimed, jumping up and down.

The two Elves nodded at the mention of their names and together shot a beam of light at the girls, starting as one but splitting off into three, piercing the girls through their hearts. The trio was once again transforming into Cute, Pretty, and Beautiful—the Magical Tutorial Goddesses!

Once the light subsided, the three girls each struck their signature poses—revealing their magical outfits that had replaced their school uniforms.

Suzu, the Cute Magical Tutorial Goddess, wore a short teal dress with a lilac sailor collar. Violet cords were wrapped around her waist, with USBs hanging loosely at her back like twin tails. Her headphones had changed into a light, mint green. She wore long, lilac socks with a dark green keyboard pattern encircling the top of her thighs. Her cropped boots were green to match and had purple video game controller buttons—joysticks, a D-pad, and face buttons—on the toes.

Noriko, the Pretty Magical Tutorial Goddess, wore a pale-yellow dress with bell sleeves and a dark green waist cincher. She wore no shoes but had matching green anklets. A necklace made of chunky, green beads lay across her bodice. Her ponytail was now held back by a thick, green band. A large nimbus-style halo floated behind her head—giving off a light purer than the sun.

Atsuko, the Beautiful Magical Tutorial Goddess, wore a loose, light blue dress—plain in its design compared to the other two Goddesses, but its fabric seemed to reflect the moving clouds in the sky. A metal tiara adorned her hair, with crystals resembling precipitation cascading down from it. She was barefoot, with nothing adorning her ankles, unlike Pretty. In her hand was a weightless, blue, glassy orb.

"Our attacks are having no effect!" Jet shouted, dodging another tree and jumping onto a lamppost. "Someone needs to enter the Deadly Omen's dimension to defeat it." He jumped once more and landed on the cobblestones in front of the girls. "Unfortunately, we used most of our power to restore your memories, so we can only send one of you!"

The Goddesses looked at one another, silently deciding who should be the first to go back to *There* after their sudden reunion.

Suzu stepped forward with her newly regained confidence as Cute.

Bone jumped away from an incoming attack, and phased into Cute's body, giving her a boost in power. Jet spiraled, dodging an attack that was almost too close, and followed him.

The Deadly Omen—sensing the Cute Magical Tutorial Goddess' sudden increase in power—aimed its next attack at her.

But before its attack could hit, Cute spread her arms wide and found herself back in *There*.

It was in There that all battles between the Goddesses and Deadly Omens took place—a barren wasteland, which only Elves, Goddesses, and the Omens could access. No mere mortals would get hurt from the results of any battle in There.

Cute adjusted her headphones and levitated off the ground, summoning holographic keyboards. She cracked her knuckles and got busy.

Any thought she had about how to defeat the Omen immediately converted itself into a programming language unknown to normal human programmers. Cute typed rapidly as the variables and functions came to her, alternating between the holograms and the physical keyboard on her thighs.

Rectangular screens of all sizes blinked on in the air, showing all sorts of information—the Omen's strengths, and its weaknesses. Utilizing her powers to the fullest like this was yet another advantage to being in There.

One by one, the screens sent out ones and zeros in the Omen's direction as Cute typed.

The Omen reached out, trying to attack Cute, but she summoned a shield. Cute's hands were a blur as she created the most powerful combination of attacks that she could think of. The Omen attempted to dodge, but soon found there was no escape—leaping away from one beam led to leaping into another. Every zero or one that pelted the Omen refracted into additional ones and zeros, causing additional damage. It hissed as its skin burned from the light show, before it finally collapsed, turning back into a small, harmless salamander.

It was then that the Deadly Omen's dimension started to dissolve, revealing Doll Park once more. Cute turned around and found herself standing next to Pretty and Beautiful.

In a flash of light, Jet and Bone emerged from her heart. However, instead of rabbits, they took on their true forms—two men in their early twenties, with pointed ears. Jet wore his long hair loose, whereas Bone had short, fluffy hair. The two men wore suits, and if not for their sudden appearance on the scene and the events that had just transpired, would probably be able to fit in as waiters at a semi-formal restaurant.

And so, the first episode of *Cute, Pretty, Beautiful: Magical Tutorial Goddesses: Heart-Throbbing Season* came to an end.

The credits started to roll.

OO2

Ugh. It's too *corny!* I can't *take* it!

I struggled to get my arms free from the blankets wrapped claustrophobically tight around me. My eyes hurt from the bright flashes of light on screen. I closed them to rub the sand out as I fumbled for the remote on the coffee table, trying to tune out the annoying theme song. After a few attempts of aiming it at the correct angle, the TV was finally off, but the remote was lost to the floor—the cavernous maw under the sofa.

Why was *that* on?

More importantly—*where am I?*

Untangling my legs, I finally stood and walked around in my pajamas—a green tank, red plaid shorts, and baggy white socks.

Faint light came in through the windows, so it was probably morning. Soon, I became acquainted with the single bedroom, the living room, kitchen, bathroom, and entryway.

What I *really* want to know is why I wasn't tucked into the bed.

Back in the kitchen, I looked over the counter and into the living room.

A pile of mail covered one section of the counter. I looked through it and realized that most of it was from Fujioka High School, and all of it was addressed to one "Kurosawa Takako."

Since this is a single bedroom apartment, I'm guessing that's me—unless I'm just a guest.

That would be the best explanation for why *I* wouldn't be tucked into the *bed,* at least.

One envelope was already open, so I skimmed through the contents. It was a letter with details about my school transfer. I looked over at the calendar and wall clock by the fridge.

It appears I am probably going to be late for the first day of my second year of high school.

When I opened and read all the mail from Fujioka High School, I realized I could do one of two things:

One: I go to school and pretend I know what's going on, and act like I had earned my place there—after all, I saw my apparent test scores. They *were* impressive, but I had no memory of ever attending classes or taking exams. How would I even fare in a classroom environment?

Or, *two:* I stay in the apartment where I woke up—and wait. After all, what if I'm *not* Kurosawa Takako, and I go to the school and run into the *actual* Takako?

OO3

Two weeks later, I chose option one after running out of storage space on my phone to download games and floorboards to count in the apartment.

That is to say, I was bored.

"My name is Kurosawa Takako. Nice to meet you." I was met with stares—some welcoming, but some as bored as my own.

"All right, Kurosawa. You'll be sitting over there." The teacher—whose name I had already forgotten—gestured to the window seat in the back row.

I was a growth emerging from the floor. A stump.

The girl in front of my assigned seat turned away from the window and looked at me, giving a cheerful grin and a slight wave.

Taking a deep breath, I was able to uproot myself from the floor and made it to my desk. The teacher took my sitting down as cue to start class.

I opened my textbook and a notebook in an attempt to appear more or less occupied...

But my gaze kept drifting from the blackboard to the fluffy, brunette hair of the girl in front of me. I couldn't help but be reminded of my dreams.

Every night since waking up to that magical girl anime, I've been having two vivid, recurring dreams.

The first was half of a conversation with a girl—well, *her* half of it, so it was more like she was *monologuing* to me. I could never see her face, and no matter how hard I tried to discern any features, a light blinded me—or she would pivot as I tried to circle around her. Her long, mousy hair would wave in an infinite breeze as she recited the same part of the conversation in every dream—sometimes more than once, but always with the same inflection:

"*Ahn,* flan is so *good!* But I'm *really* thankful for *normal* pudding, because having too much of the *fancy stuff* raises your expectations and leads to sadness when you can't always get what you *want,* you know?"

Chocolate and vanilla pudding—and flan—appeared in the air as she talked, surrounding her while floating around as though suspended from fishing line.

Flan is common in Japan, though? I've tried looking online for convenience stores that stock the pudding she's talking about...and found none near by.

Regardless, the meaning behind the words was inspirational—though I couldn't identify the girl no matter how hard I tried.

But I had to call her *something...*

Who *are* you, Flan Girl?

In the second dream, I was all alone in a dark room. I could run forever and never touch a wall or reach an exit. The only sound was my armored boots on the unknown floor.

I spun my pencil on my hand, but fumbled. It slipped off and clattered to my desk. The sound jolted me out of my trance.

I placed it in my desk to resist a second attempt—and my fingers brushed against some glossy paper.

Huh?

What's this?

Making sure no one was watching, I slipped the magazine onto my desk.

Magical Girl Monthly, it said in a friendly, bubbly font.

There was a picture of a girl, dressed in a gray sailor uniform. A flimsy black mask was on her face, and she wore knightly knee-high boots.

She stood in a wide stance, with her shoulders back, her white-gloved left hand on her hip. Her right arm was extended, index finger pointing at the reader. The girl's head was tilted, some of her black hair brushed outwards messily and a curl sticking up on top. Her brown eyes narrowed in a glare and her mouth was open. Combined, it was an intimidating expression that said, *Evildoers, beware.*

Hey, that's really funny.

This girl looks a lot like *me.*

OO4

"Did you see all the shooting stars a couple weeks ago?"

I jolted upright. "H-Huh?"

The girl sitting in front of me stared at me with big, green eyes. "Oh, sorry. Did I scare you?"

"Nn..."

"I just thought you might like to wake up for lunch, you know?"

You thought I was asleep, huh? In reality, I've been hunched over, reading *Magical Girl Monthly* throughout the majority of classes.

This seat has its perks.

I slid the magazine back into my desk and lightly touched the cover. Would it disappear if I relinquished all contact with it?

"I'm Minami Tsubasa."

"Nice to meet you..." I already know who you are.

I know your name.

Your birthday.

Your height, weight, blood type, and other *tidbits* of information.

For some reason, *every* girl in this class has a dedicated article in the magazine. If I weren't the one on the cover, I'd definitely think it was a prank.

Some sort of hazing from my new classmates—could someone have put this in my desk two weeks ago, and waited for me to find it after all this time?

At this point, I would have given up on the prank.

Really, you're trying to convince the new girl that her classmates are magical girls?

It's weird, though—like my dreams. It's so *stupid* and *impossible,* but maybe I was a magical girl in a past life—and Flan Girl was my teammate? But what happened to her? Did she lose her memories, too? Did we both die in battle and get reincarnated?

I opened the *bento* that had mysteriously appeared in my fridge this morning—*tamagoyaki,* shrimp *tempura,* broccoli, *tonkatsu,* and white rice. Whoever made it must have known I wasn't going to have a large breakfast because of my first day jitters.

Even *if* that first day ended up being two weeks after everybody else's.

Just thinking about this entire situation—waking up without memories, finding this magazine—put a heaviness in the pit of my stomach, so I closed the lid on the box and all those thoughts, and took out a small, cool thermos that contained—

"Ooh, you have *flan?*"

I looked up at Tsubasa, realizing that my thoughts had been tuning her out this entire time. "Yes..."

She blinked twice at me.

I blinked back, and that's when I realized...the long, fluffy hair, the chipper attitude...Tsubasa could be Flan Girl. "I—"

"*Oh* ho ho ho~" A haughty laugh from a few rows away switched the direction of my train of thought, killing ideas tied to the tracks that I would never be able to save.

"Don't mind her," Tsubasa whispered. "That's just Aki."

"*Just* Aki?" The girl in question strutted over and crossed her arms. Her golden hair was done up in two pointed arches on the top of her head, adding considerable height before coming down in long twin tails that almost swept the floor.

And *of course* her bangs had to come together in a lightning bolt pattern.

How fitting.

She was flanked by three other girls. Two of them looked bored and annoyed that they had been dragged into this.

Yeah, I feel the same.

"This is *Fujioka* Aki," said the girl to her left, the one who wasn't bored or annoyed. Her white, fluffy, shoulder-length pigtails bounced as she lifted her chin and glared at me with dark red eyes. "You should treat her with *respect*. She could buy your whole family two times over. Not that she would *want* to."

"*Thank* you, Hikari."

"It's my pleasure!"

Aki turned her attention to me. "Now, what is that you're eating?"

"Flan." I brought the spoon up to my lips.

Aki partially covered her mouth and laughed her signature laugh once again. "If that's all you're going to eat for lunch, you're going to get *fat!*"

"Or you'll get *sick* and have to go to a *hospital!*" said one of the other girls, her pink twin drills springing to life. Her hands were on her cheeks, and she lightly bit her pinky nails in excitement, revived from her boredom.

Shut up, Aoi, Aki said, coldly.

Aoi pouted and dropped her hands. "Let's go, Yukiko." Yukiko—a blue-haired girl with clips keeping her bangs out of her red eyes—patted Aoi on the shoulder as they walked back to their seats in the front row. She hadn't gotten a word in edgewise, and still seemed like she was annoyed—whether that annoyance would dissipate if she had an outlet for it was up in the air.

I feel for you.

"Now, where *were* we?" Aki asked. "Ah, *yes*. New girl. Throw away that *flan* and get something *healthier*. My treat!" She waved around a couple thousand yen.

Now, I have no idea how much money I have to my name, but I *refuse* to give in to peer pressure. I turned back to my flan, and before eating another spoonful, replied, "No."

"*'No'?*" she repeated, taken aback.

Yeah, you heard me.

"You don't say *no* to Fujioka Aki, *Kurosawa!*" Hikari ranted. "She's trying to be *charitable*—you should accept her offer before she tarnishes your reputation!"

"It's too *late* for that!" the rich girl laughed. "She missed the first two weeks of school. All I have to do is tap the mere *speck* that she is with one of my *designer* heels, and her reputation will be no more!"

"Stop it, Aki!" The back of Tsubasa's chair hit my desk and I jumped, spoon ringing against my teeth. She had her fists on her hips and got in Aki's face. "You really think we're just going to sit around as you bully her like you bully the rest of us?"

"Fujioka Aki is *not* a *bully*," Hikari huffed, leaning in. In a split second, she took a step back, all color drained from her face.

I wish that I could've seen the dirty look Tsubasa gave Hikari to make her cower like that—but like Flan Girl, a mass of hair obscured her expression.

Aki pointed at Tsubasa and then at me. "You're both just *jealous* that you're not as *amazing* as I am!" She clicked her tongue before doing a heel turn and strolling back to her seat. Hikari followed as fast as she could without forcing Aki to surrender her position as the leader.

"She's *amazing,* all right," I said out of the corner of my mouth.

"Don't listen to her," Tsubasa said, sitting back down.

"Never said I was." I ritualistically clapped my hands together. "I finished my flan."

"You sure showed her!" a new voice chimed in from my right.

I turned and saw two girls.

One was tall with short, light green hair, a shoulder length cowlick starting from her bangs. A dark green clip with a bow resembling two leaves stuck up out of her hair. She stood arms akimbo with a huge grin on her face.

The other was a ponytailed redhead with orange eyes and freckles. She was definitely the girl who gave me what I assumed was a compliment, as she was bent over in a perfect ninety-degree angle at her waist, arms crossed but with a giddy look on her face.

"Uh...thanks?"

"I'm Yoshida Hotaru, and this is Hayashi Nana," the redhead continued. Hotaru sat down in the empty seat next to me, backwards, and slouched as she crossed her arms once more. "Man, Aki's sure annoying, isn't she? Always taking every chance she can to rub her wealth in everyone's face, doing that stupid *ho ho ho* laugh, like *what—* is she *Santa?* But you'll probably get used to her after..." She trailed off.

"A semester?" Nana suggested, sitting on the desk that Hotaru stole her chair from.

"I was *gonna* say *never...*"

Hotaru and Nana shared a laugh.

It didn't escape my attention that Aki left the classroom in a huff, tailed by her clique.

"So, who are her minions?" Once again, I have to pretend that I don't know anything about them. I wish that I never read *Magical Girl Monthly.*

"The one with pigtails who defended Aki is Nakajima Hikari. She's the class president, and her mother is apparently a powerful CEO," Nana explained.

"'Apparently'?"

You were all in the same class as her for your first year, right?

Shouldn't you *know* by now?

"Well, that's what Hikari always *says,*" Tsubasa added. "She never specifies the company—so who knows if she's telling the truth?"

Can't you just research CEOs who are mothers with daughters? Or CEOs who share her surname?

Hotaru laced her fingers together and stretched. There was an audible *crack.* "Hikari also plans to start her own corporation after graduating."

Hm. High hopes.

"The one with the blue hair who didn't say anything is Hideki Yukiko. She transferred here last year in the second semester." Tsubasa tilted her head. "Something about stalkers at her last school?"

"Yeah, the details are kinda fuzzy on *that* one," Hotaru sighed. "To be honest, every time I've talked to her, she's been kinda *boooring.*"

Isn't that a contradiction? Anyone with stalkers probably has stories to tell, right?

"And finally," Tsubasa said, bringing her hands to her cheeks, teasingly, "the one who seemed a bit too excited when she brought up hospitals is Sasaki Aoi." She then rolled her eyes and dropped her palms, resting her elbows on my desk. "She's *really* only part of the group because *Yukiko* is."

"Really?"

Hotaru nodded, ponytail bobbing. "Yeah, Yukiko made a *big* deal about it when Aki, Hikari, and Manami approached her to join. 'Sure, *I'll* join. But only if *Aoi* can join, too.' She really gave an ultimatum for friendship! Like, who even does that?"

"And who's Manami?" I asked—even though I already knew the answer.

Nana, Hotaru, and Tsubasa craned their necks to look at the other side of the room. My gaze followed.

"Oh, she's probably at the school store with Chou!" Tsubasa announced. "You'll get to meet the two of them later. They're a *blast!*"

"Oh, okay."

Awkward silence.

Nana fidgeted with her *ahoge,* curling it around her finger, her lip twitching as if she were keeping something inside. Unable to keep it in any longer, she quickly blurted out, "Raw wheat, raw rice, raw eggs!"

"Huh?" I blinked. "Are those your nicknames for Fujioka's lackeys?"

Hotaru sighed and patted Nana on the shoulder—or at least, as high up as she could reach while still sitting down. "Nah, she just resorts to tongue twisters when she can't think of anything else to say."

"That's..." Unique.

Hotaru stood and gave Nana one last hard pat on the back before going back to her seat. "Talk later, Takako?"

"Um, sure..."

Tsubasa leaned on my desk. "So, *did* you see the shooting stars?"

"Uh, no. I was asleep."

"Oh, that's too bad! I just happened to see them—didn't hear anything about it in advance. They were so beautiful. It was the night before school started. When I saw the first few, I kept watching, and kinda...stayed up until morning..." She smiled, sheepishly. "I was almost late, but it was definitely worth it!"

"Better than being two weeks late, right?"

Tsubasa let out a laugh like wind chimes. "That's true, that's true!"

She continued to go on about stars, space, and her dreams, and when required I supplied her with a *Hm* or *Is that so?* until break was over, and class started up again.

OO5

Class ended for the day, so I took out *Magical Girl Monthly* to continue reading, moving on from the information on my classmates to a page that introduces the *concept* of *monsters*.

Yes, monsters.

And according to the magazine, some monsters will *appear* shortly. Ha.

But really, if I'm to believe that magical girls are real—which given the evidence, I have no choice *but* to believe—it would only make sense they would need something to fight.

Or they exist because something needs to be defeated.

Which came first, the monster or the—

"What are you reading?"

I jolted up from the magazine. "Huh?"

"What are you reading?" the girl repeated in the same exact tone. She had short, dark blue hair in a bob that framed her pale face. Her dark blue eyes were unblinking. She was none other than Kawaguchi Youko—and if not for the magazine, I would not have known this.

"Oh, it's..." There's no way I can tell her the truth. She either wouldn't believe me, or would freak out—which, judging by her monotone, *would* be a sight to see. The boys on cleaning duty would no doubt run to assist her. "Nothing. Just a magazine."

"Magazines aren't allowed at school."

"They aren't?"

"Correct."

I blinked. She's not going to *confiscate* it or anything, is she? If she flicked through it and saw the article on herself or one of the other girls in class...with all that information, there's no *doubt* I would be labeled a deviant.

I'd be ostracized!

"I won't tell anyone." Youko took a few steps towards her desk, then added over her shoulder, *This time, at least.* She picked up her bag from the hook on her desk and walked out of the classroom.

I guess I'll call it a day, too.

I flipped the magazine to one of Nana's pages and tore off a strip—the outer margin—puzzled when it came off a *bit* neater than I had anticipated.

Still jagged, but the width was pretty consistent considering it hadn't been perforated.

It was dark green and glossy, covered in a pattern that at first looked like randomly placed lines, but was really thick grass, with leaves hidden behind the blades in the foreground.

I packed my bag—making sure to include the magazine—and slung it over my shoulder, hiding the scrap paper by gripping the bag's strap.

Outside, the sky was gray, and some drops of rain were already on the window.

Great, I didn't bring an umbrella. Maybe someone forgot one in the rack, or I can ask a senior to share with me.

oo6

"What the hell *are* these things?" Hotaru shouted. She backed herself against the side of the school with Nana, away from four large blobs.

The blobs were blue, and had a consistency similar to drops of water—though with their size, the surface tension needed to keep their forms would be impossible.

And of course, these were only four blobs that had their attention focused on the two girls—there were twenty on the school grounds at *least.*

"How am *I* supposed to know?! *Run* for it!"

They started running back to the school's entrance, but the redhead wasn't as fast as her friend—and was soon surrounded. "*God,* this is so *stupid!*" Frustrated, she punched one of the offending blobs, and it absorbed the attack with a *glorp!*

"Hotaru!" Nana shouted, turning back to see her friend in trouble.

"Just go without me!" Hotaru cried out as she was sucked into the blob.

Nana took a few bouncy steps in place, torn between running and trying to save her best friend.

This was when *I* exited from the school's main entrance and saw the large blobs—Water Droplets—on the campus.

Everything the magazine said...really *was* true?

"Hey! Takako! *Buddy!*" Nana shouted, running up to me. "Get back inside! We've gotta get...I don't know, a *teacher?* The *headmaster?*" She pulled at her long lock of hair, twisting it around her finger.

I couldn't move. The Water Droplets—about chest height—mesmerized me as they swallowed lingering students left and right.

One of them lurched towards us, and Nana pulled me out of my trance and into the school, slamming the doors shut. The Water Droplet pressed up against the doors, and—as if it decided that it was too much effort to grow digits capable of pulling them open—went on its way.

Hopefully not to get reinforcements.

Nana slumped down against the shoe lockers, finally catching her breath.

"*So...*" I sat down next to her. "I take it this isn't normal?"

"Was it normal at your *old* school?"

I shrugged.

"This is like something out of one of Tsubasa's weird dreams..." Nana whispered. She turned to me and waved her hands in panic. "No, not one of *those* dreams! Tsubasa's not like that, I swear! Well, I don't *think* she is, but... *Agh!*" She ruffled her hair in frustration. "The guest next door is a guest that eats a *lot* of persimmons!"

"I don't think there's anything wrong with weird dreams. I mean...my dreams for the past two weeks have been strange. Doesn't *everyone* have weird dreams occasionally?"

Nana's answer flickered across her face: Yes, she does, but she doesn't want to say what they are.

I mean, I don't blame her—we only met today, and dreams *are* kind of personal.

Bang! Bang!

The Water Droplets mindlessly—*are* they mindless?—circled back to the school's main entrance after either absorbing or chasing everyone off campus.

Everyone except for us, at least.

"I don't think the doors are gonna hold." Nana got into a crouch, stretching her hamstrings. "How fast are you at running?"

"Eh."

"Not the answer I was looking for...but *okay!* Let's *go!*" She grabbed my hand and we made it to the end of the lockers, but stopped when I let go. "Takako? What's wrong?" She opened her hand, revealing that torn strip of green paper I stealthily passed to her. "What's this?"

"*Don't* lose it." I faced the doors, which were now blocked completely by the monsters. "Let's go."

"Out there?"

"No." I extended my arms outward, willing a portal into existence in front of the doors.

"What is *that?*"

"I, Takako, take this task of delivering justice to this evil in the form of another hero. Please, let me guide her on her journey to her true destiny—protector of this Earth. I don my mask and responsibility as her mentor. I, Takako, now sleep as I wear this mask—and my true power awakens!"

While reciting this speech I memorized from *Magical Girl Monthly*, I levitated in fetal position as my school uniform melted away. I somersaulted in midair a few times, then landed back on my feet. Mirroring the pose on the magazine cover, I pointed at the Droplets. My outfit had completely changed to that gray *seifuku* from the magazine. I turned to face Nana.

Before she could once again ask what was going on, the strip of paper slid from her grasp and encircled her wrist. A white flower sprouted from it, and green light coursed up her arm from the corsage, enveloping her whole body.

"And what was *that?*" she asked when the light dissipated. No longer in her school uniform, she stood before me, barefoot, dressed in a green skirt and leggings, an asymmetrical top revealing her bare midriff. Suspenders connected her shirt and skirt like vines, and a choker of daisies encircled her throat. The same hair clip she had been wearing before on top of her head—it must be important enough to her that the transformation kept it.

I knelt down in front of her as her loyal knight—hand over my heart, head down. The sudden formality confused her. If she had looked closer, she probably would've thought that I had passed out.

However, my mind was racing—and I was acting as the bridge

between this world and the next.

The doors weren't going to hold any longer. Nana tried to pick me up, but I was rooted to the floor, a statue—not out of fear this time, but out of power.

Before any of the monsters could break into the school, Nana jumped into the portal, and I willed it to close behind her.

OO7

The whole world had an unnatural blue tint that somehow felt heavy—similar to the change in lighting and pressure before a storm but *not quite.* I looked down at my hands and realized I was translucent.

Nana was in front of me, facing what appeared to be a wide river. She took a few steps but stopped.

On the opposite bank, there was a low wall, and beyond that were the Water Droplets, jiggling as they wandered aimlessly.

Even further away, I could see a levitating lily pad. Condensation gathered on the blue-green leaf, causing it to sag under the weight. When the angle became too great, a Water Droplet slid from the leaf to the ground, letting out a *splash.*

I stepped up beside Nana and crossed my arms. "Huh. *That* doesn't look *good,*" I stated.

"Gah!" she exclaimed, jolting a foot into the air.

I ignored this. "Well? Go on."

Nana blinked. "What?"

"You're a magical girl. Go on." I pumped my fist. "*Fight.*"

"But...I don't know how? I mean, yeah, I *know* how to run fast and do fancy jumps...and I guess if I needed to, I could throw a bunch of punches and kicks? But these are *monsters,* Takako! They don't play by any rules I know!"

I gave Nana's shoulder a pat—sighing at her newbie attitude, but also at the fact that my translucent hand merely phased through and fell back at my side. Looking up at her with my most determined look, I raised my other hand in a thumbs up. "You can do it."

And with that, I faded away.

"Well, that wasn't helpful. Like, *at all.*"

Gee, *thanks.* I'm still here—just invisible and intangible, you know?

Nana swallowed the lump in her throat, crouched, and launched herself to the opposite bank, perching on the wall. When her feet touched the ground on the other side, the Water Droplets came for her.

She closed her eyes and brought her arms up to block the impact that never came—tall grass and flowers sprung forth from the ground, shielding her from and damaging the Droplets.

Nana opened her eyes in time to see the foliage retreating back into the ground. The Water Droplets that had been on the verge of attack were a considerable distance away, and would have been further if not for another low wall. Nana looked down at her hands. "*I did that?*"

There was a *schlorp-schlorp* and she looked back up. The attack had merely stalled the Droplets—and they were coming back for more.

She charged at the monsters, flailing her arms—plants rapidly grew out of the ground in front of her with every gesture. One after another, the Water Droplets became puddles, quickly absorbed by the ground. However, the lily pad replaced each one with another Droplet.

Nana looked down, noticing each small victory resulted in something appearing. "I-Is that...*pudding?*"

I made myself visible and picked up one of the pudding cups. I turned it in my hand. *Interesting*—there was no branding on it. "Mm, yeah."

"Why?" Nana blinked before attacking a few more Droplets. "Will it make me stronger?"

I pulled off the red lid and made a quick gesture, like spinning a pen, to summon a spoon. Taking a bite of the vanilla pudding, I replied with the spoon in my mouth, *I guess.*

"Why are *you* the one eating it, then?!"

I shrugged as I took a few more bites and scraped the sides of the cup to get the last of it out. "I'm hungry."

That's what I get for only eating flan for lunch, I guess.

Nana gave me a frustrated sigh. "*Okay,* then. Can you *maybe* tell me how to stop these monsters from reappearing when they *die?*"

"Yeah." I picked up another pudding cup. "You have to destroy where they're coming from."

"You mean the lily pad?"

"Yeah." I examined the cup I just picked up. "Ooh, *chocolate!*"

Nana's shoulders slumped in defeat. "You've got powers too, Takako. Why do *I* have to do all the work?"

"My powers are different than yours," I replied, shrugging as I tore off the lid and took a spoonful.

I guess, I added through a bite.

"'I guess,'" Nana repeated, just loud enough for me to hear. She leapt to the hovering lily pad, arms outstretched. Buds shot out from her hands and blossomed into flowers midair. The lily pad wilted, as though its nutrients were stolen.

I tossed away my empty cup before fading out and reappearing next to the lily pad. I watched it collapse into itself, leaving behind a four-pack of vanilla pudding. "Ooh, *nice.*" Because there was no way for me to eat all of that pudding in one sitting, I followed the advice of *Magical Girl Monthly* and lifted my arm as if I were wearing a cape—tucking the snack away for later in some sort of pocket dimension dedicated to pudding.

A pudding dimension.

Nana jumped to two more lily pads, destroying them and some Water Droplets as they spawned from them—allowing me to pick up two more packs of vanilla pudding.

However—

One Water Droplet got the best of her—and sent her flying off the platform to the swarm below.

That's not good...

Nana fell, back against a wall, as the Water Droplets buffeted against her like a rain storm.

I thought back to everything I had read in the magazine about her powers. "*Hey!* Use your *finisher!*"

She looked up at me in a daze. "What...would *that* be?"

"Run!"

Nana clawed at the slimy wall until she was finally able to stand. She pushed her way through the Water Droplets—as she gained speed, thick grass grew underfoot, repelling the Water Droplets before retreating back into the ground.

Water Droplets that repelled from the grass, only to bounce off their fellow Droplets and back into the grass, were destroyed on contact, leaving vanilla and chocolate pudding in their wake, along with...

"Flan?"

"*Flan!*" I appeared next to Nana, cupped my hands together, and picked up the dessert, holding it close to my heart.

"That was on the ground. *Please* tell me you're not gonna *eat* it."

"It was *hovering*. Besides, it's more *symbolic* than anything."

Magical Girl Monthly actually explained this to me—I'm not a *deviant* who would just pick up any dessert she sees and eat it. The pudding and flan aren't *really* pudding and flan. They're a type of energy that takes the appearance of these desserts to make them enticing enough to pick up.

Chocolate pudding to heal injuries, and vanilla to get stronger—flan, on the other hand? Didn't say—only that it was important.

And who am I to question an omnipotent magazine?

But even if I don't directly question it, I can still wonder to myself—*why* did it choose this form?

I don't know.

Anyway, this mysterious energy that can be used to heal magical girls *or* make them stronger—just so happens to double as a tasty snack!

"I'm not even gonna ask..." Nana looked around as I picked up more of the desserts. "So, what now? I beat all the monsters, and the lily pads are gone."

I closed my eyes and put a finger to my temple. "No, I can sense three more lily pads in a cavern below us."

"You've *gotta* be *kidding* me..."

"There's also a giant Water Droplet."

Really, I'm not sensing anything—just recalling what I read from the Water Droplets' page in the magazine.

Nana vaulted over a wall mid-groan, landing near a lily pad.

You look energized.
I guess the pudding worked.

008

A boy who had to be ten years old lay prone in the Darkness, with one arm outstretched, reaching for a large, glowing blue marble. He looked through his fluffy, dark blue bangs with luminous yellow-green eyes. Closing one eye to focus, he pouted and shot the marble into the ring. As it ricocheted off of a few smaller marbles, its surface returned to a dull, blue finish.

Clink! Clink! Clink!

"It's not *fair!*" He stood and kicked the black sack that held the rest of the marbles, scattering them. Each was a different shade of blue taken from the world, but with none of the life that came with the color.

The boy's pointed ears twitched.

Kenji—a disembodied baritone voice emanated from the shadows. "What seems to be the matter?"

"My marbles broke!" Kenji picked up a handful of the glass orbs, clacking them together.

"They don't *appear* to be damaged." Wisps of Darkness swirled around the ring, emphasizing the playing field. "Start another round, or play a different game."

"But I *wanted* to play with the *special* marbles!" Kenji bent down and grabbed onto his battle axe. He chopped the last blue marble he had launched, shattering it.

009

Upon the destruction of the final Droplet—a behemoth that towered over us—a blue door appeared. Despite its size—twice the height of a regular door, and as wide as my arm span—it matched the rest of the world to the extent that it almost went unnoticed by us.

"Is that the exit?"

"Yeah." I picked up all the pudding and flan that the monster dropped. "When we go through that door, we'll be back at school—and no one will remember the Water Droplets."

I hesitated before adding, *Probably.*

"*Probably?*"

"I mean, a bunch of students got absorbed by them. Would *you* forget something like that?"

"Takako, what's going on? I mean *really,* what *was* all that?"

"The Water Droplets came from...somewhere. The sky, maybe?" The sky makes sense. I mean, it *did* seem like it was starting to rain in our world. "I don't know," I continued. "We're just living in a magical girl anime now. Or something."

"Then...there's a *moral* to all this? Are we supposed to *learn* something?"

One cup tumbled from the top of the pile as I tried to shrug, but

Nana swooped in and caught it. "Your guess is as good as mine."

Not all magical girl anime have morals, right?

"So, will there be other monsters?" Nana furrowed her brow. "I don't think I want to fight again..."

Too bad. You have no choice.

"I mean, yes—I think it's bad that there're monsters, and they *should* be fought by *someone,* but...I just don't have it *in* me to fight again, y'know?"

I looked her in the eyes as I stored all the desserts I was holding in the pudding dimension. She passed me the cup she had caught. "No, I don't know."

Nana slumped in defeat at my response.

Hey, at least I'm honest.

"But you don't have to fight again for a while. I mean—there *are* magical girls besides us."

"Really? Then why don't we form a team?" She grasped my hands between her own—I guess the power of the pudding made me tangible?

Eagerly, she suggested, *We can fight the monsters together! All of us!*

"I'm simply a Mascot to cheer you on so you may fulfill your true potential." I awkwardly slid my hands out of her grip. "I can only provide the power for one transformation at a time."

Besides my own, that is, I explained.

Nana blinked. "I guess that makes sense..." She started walking to the door. "So, who's gonna be next?"

I stopped in my tracks. "Huh?"

"Who're you gonna give powers to next?"

I opened and closed my mouth in a silent stutter.

Like a fish.

Nana walked through the door before I could fudge an answer, and found herself back in the school's entryway. I looked up at her through my eyelashes, groggily, in fetal position.

"Whoa, are you okay?!" She fell to her knees and shook me awake—because apparently one can't be awake with her eyes closed.

"Yeah, I'm fine," I grumbled, dragged to my feet faster than I would have liked. We were both in our school uniforms again, so there was no worry about anyone seeing us as magical girls—and by extension, no need for her to pull me up that fast.

"*Nana!*"

We looked at the doors. There were no more Water Droplets—instead, a pissed off Hotaru stood there, catching her breath.

A soaked cat.

She squeezed water out of her ponytail like wringing out a towel before flicking it back over her shoulder.

"Oh. It's raining." I looked past her to the outside world. It was gray and dreary compared to the blue world we had just left. I resisted rubbing my eyes to adjust to the different lighting.

"No, it's *pouring!*" Hotaru walked in, *squelching* with every step. "Nana, I *know* you ran to get your umbrella so we could share, but *friends* are supposed to get caught in the rain *together,*" she whined. "It's not—" She cut herself off with a sneeze.

I stated the obvious: *You'd better get into something dry.*

Hotaru nodded in agreement before sneezing again.

"My my, someone must be talking about you!" Nana teased.

"Shut up and get me my gym clothes."

With the phrase *Red pajamas, yellow pajamas, brown pajamas* rolling off her tongue, Nana kicked off her shoes and ran to the stairs in her sock feet.

OIO

I'm a magical girl. A *real-life* magical girl.

Click!

I stepped into my apartment and locked the door behind me.

After putting the umbrella I borrowed on the rack next to my own, I opened my bag to take out *Magical Girl Monthly*—but discovered it wasn't there. Turning on the lights, I upended my bag as I walked to the coffee table, making a mess of textbooks and notebooks to ensure the magazine wasn't sandwiched between any pages.

No, wait.

That would be *impossible.*

The magazine is bigger than anything else that's in my bag.

I sighed and walked all the way over to the TV—the remote has been lost to the sofa for these past two weeks—then walked to the kitchen.

Another episode of that anime—*Cute, Pretty, Beautiful* whatever—that I had woken up to was on.

I mean, it's kinda funny if I give it some thought. I started a new "episode" in my life by waking up to a series premiere.

But the universe has to be playing a trick on me, right?

This channel that my TV is permanently stuck to without the remote is broadcasting nothing but magical girl anime.

I guess *this* is my life now.

I looked up at the show as I started percolating coffee. The magical girls were *crying*—screaming *passionately*—about the *powers* of *love* and *friendship* to a fourth magical girl dressed like a stage magician's assistant. She stood atop a tower of brambles and twisted metal, looking down at the team with boring, beige eyes, blinking once as if to say, *I'm bored.*

"I'm bored," she said, tilting her head. Her purple hair framed her face, sharply cutting it away from the rest of her body at the neck. "Call me when you're ready to fight me for real."

And with that, she took one step off the back of the tower and plummeted down. "Gorgeous!"

I blinked. I mean, the backwards swan dive *was* gorgeous, I guess—but how would you be able to see it? It was clearly at an angle that only the audience could see, and—oh, that's the character's *name* you're screaming, okay.

"No," Bone said. "She's gone."

"B-But," Cute cried, "why would she do this? She's supposed to be a Magical Tutorial Goddess, too!"

"Unfortunately, she's let power go to her head," Jet replied. "She's a Deadly Omen Finder now."

I walked to the fridge to see what's for dinner. Ever since I woke up here, the fridge and cabinets have restocked themselves. Of course, I stopped questioning it after the second time I noticed.

I mean, whatever force breaking into my apartment with the *sole purpose* of providing me with the fixings for a balanced diet—and sometimes entire meals—can't be entirely bad, right?

Though when I opened the fridge tonight, I had to do some digging to find ingredients for dinner—they were bricked behind a wall of all the pudding and flan I had picked up in the other world.

That's right. I counted.

So...being a magical girl might *actually* be a problem...

EPISODE TWO

YOUKO FLARES

OOI

Magical Girl Monthly was mocking me—I was certain of it.

The day after the battle, I found it back in my desk—as though it had never left.

And it's been there every day since.

I glared down at the cover.

"Oh my God! I still can't get over that magical girl last week!"

I lifted my head and started eavesdropping on the conversation at the front of the room.

Takakuwa Manami—resident gal. Her pink hair was up in two galaxy buns. She was a walking dress code violation, sitting sideways on her best friend's desk, legs crossed.

"Yeah! She was so amazing, *nya!*"

Okuma Chou—resident cat girl. With brunette pig tails and a yellow bow pinned to the back of her head, I couldn't help but notice that her silhouette resembles her favorite animal.

"*Really* just can't believe that, like, magical girls are actually *real,* y'know? Like, if we were in junior high, that'd be really cool. I'd *def* wanna be one! But I mean..." Manami crossed her arms. "We're in high school, and we're gonna have to worry about *exams* and *university* soon..." She nibbled on her thumbnail. "Just kinda *sad* that I missed my chance..."

You didn't miss your chance. None of you have.

I looked over to Nana. She was slumped over her desk, face buried in her arms. She hadn't seemed exhausted at all after the fight—I mean, she *did* have the energy to run up and down the stairs to get Hotaru's gym clothes.

But since then, it seems like she's been steadily losing energy.

And today—she seemed *completely* drained.

"If you're feeling sick, go home," Hotaru said, resting her hand on Nana's back. "Or at *least* wear a mask so no one else gets whatever you've caught."

"Mm..." Nana turned her head to look up at her, but then buried her face again. "Not sick. Just tired."

"C'mon, Nana." Hotaru leaned over Nana, giving her shoulder a couple nudges, trying to rouse her. "Don't cha wanna get somethin' from the vending machine?"

"Just get me an energy drink. The blue one," Nana groaned. As an afterthought, she mumbled, *Please...*

"Kay kay!" Hotaru cheered, running out of the classroom.

I turned my attention back to Manami and Chou. They had moved on from sharing their woes about being too old to be magical girls, to discussing the possible logical explanation of a magical girl.

"So, like, it's *gotta* be a publicity stunt or something, right?"

I *guess* that would make sense. After all, *Cute, Pretty, Beautiful* whatever started recently. If someone ever catches me while I'm transformed, that'd be a good cover story, too.

Yeah, I'm the new character, *Lovely,* from the hit show *Cute, Pretty, Beautiful: Magical—*

"Hmm..." Chou brought her hands up to her cheeks, fingers curled to imitate paws. She tilted not just her head, but her whole body to the side—how she stayed in her seat was a mystery to me. "I *dunno.* It seemed pretty real! *Too* real to be faked, *nya!*"

Hey—I raised my voice just enough for them to hear me across the room. They turned to face me. "What channel was that on? The real-life magical girl. I think I missed it."

Manami blinked at me and tapped the corner of her glossed lips, looking at the ceiling as she thought about it. "I first saw it on the local news station. Their source was that one site. *You* know—*that* site. It was uploaded *anonymously.*"

"I saw it on the kids' channel!" Chou interjected. "It was an alert that interrupted my usual programming!"

I thought there was gonna be an earthquake, she added.

Is my TV stuck on the kids' channel? That would explain the magical girl anime...

Manami nodded at Chou. "Oh yeah, it's been on a *bunch* of different channels this week. All the reports are *'unsure'* of what really happened." A flicker of inspiration lit up in her eyes. "Oh! I've actually got the tab saved on my phone! Wanna see?"

Before I could answer, Manami slid off Chou's desk and skipped over to me, thumbing through a streaming app. Chou stood and followed. Manami presented her phone to me—weighed down by charms—and pressed play.

That's Nana.

That's so *obviously* Nana—dressed in green, fighting Water Droplets in the street, just outside the school.

Why hasn't anyone recognized her?

Wait...

How was this even *filmed?*

We were in that *other* world...so why is the video showing the street in front of the school?

I said nothing and continued to watch in silence, hoping that my shock wasn't visible.

With every Water Droplet defeated, the clouds above unleashed a torrential downpour—as if the gods wanted to show their displeasure towards that *one spot* in particular.

The fight continued, until the entire sky was falling in the form of cats and dogs—leaning more towards dogs, though, since there wasn't anything graceful about how this rain fell to the ground—and Nana disappeared into the mist.

"So, who filmed this?" Flan Girl? Are you around?

"Huh?" Manami tilted her head.

"The video. I can't see anyone in the video who's also recording.

They're all just running around, screaming in terror. So, this has to be the only video of her and the monsters, right? So, who posted it?"

"She *said* it's *anony-mouse*," Chou grumbled, though her decision to use a pun right then and there detracted from the desired effect.

"Right, sorry."

"So, some news sites started getting calls and stuff. Not about the magical girls, but about the weather. The people of Fujioka have spoken—and they are *pissed*. Like, *yeah*, it *was* gonna rain that day. But not that *hard!* Anyway, they were looking for video evidence of the bad weather, and found this."

I stared at Manami. "So *why* are they believing it's real?"

"It's 'cause they were getting complaints from our area that the weather was wrong from *Time A* to *Time B*—but this is the only video showing anything other than what was forecast!"

I decided not to argue, and instead let her continue.

"Now, the people in the video—who, might I add, have been identified and *just* completed background checks and have like, *no* acting experience—*came forward,* except for the magical girl and videographer. And these people—these *people,* not *actors*—they *claim* that they have absolutely *no memory* of being attacked by the monsters. Y'know, *even though* it was *caught on camera!* Nope! They just remember it being cloudy, and then the next moment they were caught in more rain than they expected!"

"Excuse me." We turned to face Youko. "Phones aren't allowed in school."

Manami blinked, and then looked down at her hand, still holding what seemed to be more charms than phone. She quickly hid it behind her. "*Whoopsie!*" The charms tinkled together—a wind chime of pop culture and cuteness. "Won't happen again, Yo-Yo!"

Youko nodded and went back to her seat.

"So, who do you think the magical girl is?" I asked, trying to get us back on track.

"Oh, she could be *anyone,*" Manami replied.

"Yeah!" Chou chimed in.

"Someone in this classroom, then?"

Manami snorted and Chou giggled.

"Whaaaat?" Manami asked, flicking a tear out of her eye once she regained her composure. "*Definitely* not. She's probably a-a-a-an *actress* or something!"

Chou puffed out her cheeks. "She *could be* a high schooler..."

"I mean—*yeah,* she *could* be. But hey, this is a *publicity* stunt! They'd sooner pay someone who *used to be* a high schooler to play pretend as a magical girl than get someone from this room—y'know, an *actual* high schooler—to fill the role."

Nana jolted upright as Hotaru pressed an icy can against her forehead. "They were out of the blue, so I got you green."

"*Thanks.*" Nana pouted. "I hate the green."

OO2

I walked downstairs, trying to get an idea of where everything's located in the school.

Four floors.

No classrooms on the ground level. Bathrooms on every floor, in the same corner of the building. Twelve classrooms split between floors two, three, and four. My class—2-C—is on the third floor at the front of the building. I could easily see the front entrance from my window seat.

The cooking and sewing rooms are on the third floor, along with a computer lab across from 2-C.

Two elevators at the building's rear have access to all four floors.

Something interesting to note—that I don't fully understand myself—is that there is no single stairwell that accesses all four floors. To reach the roof from the ground floor, one must traverse through the halls, alternating the stairs taken, until reaching their final destination.

And it's not like one stairwell is closed off from the other below it—there are balconies, so you can see the other stairwells below!

Who *designed* this school?

I'm getting dizzy...

In the middle of making my mental map of everything, I rounded a corner and bumped into someone who was just standing there.

"Excuse me," I muttered, not even looking at them and trying to get by as fast as possible.

"'*Excuse*' you?" Aki parroted.

Oh no.

"No, stop walking. I'm *talking* to you!"

Yukiko and Aoi blocked my path.

"Turn around." Yukiko didn't *command* me, per se—but I still felt a chill run down my spine.

Ah, so *this* is the type of girl whose ultimatum is accepted without hesitation.

"You heard her," Aoi added, hair springing wildly about her as she nodded her head in Yukiko's direction.

I did as I was told. "I'm sorry, Fujioka, I—"

Aki took two steps forward before confidently placing a hand on her hip and flipping one of her over-the-top pigtails.

Do they even qualify as pigtails, though? Shouldn't pigtails be short? These are more like...giraffe tails? No, they have long necks, not tails. Snake tails?

Seriously, though. Why does she feel the need to have her hair almost touching the floor? And what's with those weird, pointy loop things? Those must take a lot of preparation, hair spray, and other products in the morning to stay up all day...

"Ah *hem!*" Hikari tapped her foot, waiting for my response.

I blinked. Apparently, I had been too distracted by Aki's hair to bother listening to what she was saying.

What could Aki have said?

Something about bumping into her?

Does she want me to kneel down and kiss her shoe?

Hm... How to get her off my back in such a way that I won't have to listen to why she pulled me over—or another spiel about how I didn't listen to the first spiel?

Well...they *do* say the truth will set you free!

"Oh, sorry about that, Fujioka!" I patted the back of my head, trying to be casual. "I was just..." I have to play my cards right. "I was distracted by your hair! Did you do something new with it?"

"Why...*yes!*" Aki gave her signature laugh. "*Yes,* in fact! I'm surprised someone like *you* would even notice it! I've started using a new shampoo that I had imported from *France!*" She whipped both pigtails at me in some attempt to waft the scent in my direction. "Do you smell that? *La Puanteur.* That's *French* for *The Panther!* It has a strong scent that only the most *discerning* noses can appreciate—a mix of over a *hundred* herbs and essential oils. Perhaps you've heard of it?"

"I can't say that I have," I squeaked, discreetly wiping a tear from my eye.

"Oh, poor *you!* Of *course* you haven't! It's *very* exclusive." Aki closed the distance and flicked my cowlick. "It was developed by my favorite artist—you've probably never heard of him. They did a limited run before discontinuing it. Only *a thousand* bottles were made!" She spun me around to face Yukiko and Aoi, so fast that I almost dropped my bag. I felt her fingers combing through my hair, poking and prodding away at my roots. My phrasing may seem like it was annoying or even painful, but...it actually felt really nice. It was a gentle act compared to the rest of her personality.

Aoi swayed side to side, shoulder occasionally brushing against Yukiko's, though Yukiko didn't seem to notice, instead looking off to the side at the blank wall, a neutral expression on her face. She fidgeted with one of the clips that kept her hair out of her eyes.

"Look at all of your split ends!" Aki exclaimed. "And the way it's *styled* in general is absolutely *dreadful!* Who *did* this to you?"

"Uh, I—"

"That was *rhetorical.*" She spun me around once more. "Aoi." She reached out and was handed a sanitizing wipe.

Wow. You think my hair is so bad that you wouldn't even wait for me to leave *before* you clean your hands? *That's* how it is, *huh?*

"Actually, it's not *entirely* rhetorical." She finished her right hand and went to her left. Instead of using the wipe like I would, Aki went about sanitizing each finger individually, using the edge to get under every *perfectly manicured* nail, ending with her pinky. Aoi reached out for the soiled wipe, before shoving it into a portable trash bag. "Let *Hikari* know so she can inform me *never* to hire your stylist."

Stylist?

"After all, I would *never* want my *amazing* hair to end up like *yours!*

It's just *horrible* compared to mine! So *dry,* with no *thought* behind the style!" She laughed. "It's like you just rolled out of *bed* with it looking like that!"

"That's because I *did.*"

"*What?*" The expression on her face was a combination of shock from me talking back to her, and a laugh about to bubble out from me admitting the truth of my haircare routine.

Okay, I admit that I brush my hair to the best of my ability. It's not *my* fault that genetics or whatever dictated that it sticks up in places that make my head look like a burnt octo-dog. I don't *really* look at my hair after rolling out of bed and think, *Good enough.*

Most days.

Regardless, even if that *is* the truth, it probably wasn't good to accidentally blurt that out to the school's bully.

I quickly backpedaled, thinking of how to turn this into a boast and earn myself a point against her in this popularity game. "I'm *my own* stylist. I was going for something—what's the *French* word for it?— *haute couture? Avant-garde?*"

Aki opened and closed her mouth, lost for words and—for once— her laugh. Finally, she turned on her heel and left with a sneer, followed by her loyal entourage.

I walked in the opposite direction—past the shoe lockers, past the library, and to the other stairwell.

I looked up at the alternating flights of stairs, and couldn't help but sigh.

There's probably no one on the roof at this time of day, making it the perfect place to read *Magical Girl Monthly* in peace—but judging by the intricate route to get there, who knows how long I'd have?

OO3

"Why can't we have any light here?" Kenji asked, despite being able to see everything perfectly in his own realm of shadows.

Because we are beings of the Darkness—the same baritone voice as before responded. "We have no use for it, as light goes against everything we stand for. Light *may* create shadows—but when there is too much light, shadows cannot exist. The *Darkness* cannot exist."

Kenji dragged his battle axe against the ground in some attempt to create sparks. "But I want a *fire!*" he shouted, before throwing his axe in the general direction of the voice. It clattered to the ground, though its sound seemed to resonate from the opposite direction. "I want to *burn* things!"

There was a pause where the voice was lost in thought, before saying, "Then perhaps an exception can be made."

Kenji saw his axe slide back to him from nowhere—a small matchbox resting on the blade.

The boy let out a happy gasp and he picked up the box.

"The Darkness has given you this gift—as anything that burns in the light of fire will soon return to shadows and nothingness. Don't say that the Darkness has never given you anything in return for your servitude."

Kenji took one match out of the box and examined it. "How does it work?" he inquired.

Met with silence, he believed he was alone again until a tendril of shadow slid the match from his grasp and quickly scratched it against the striker strip.

Kenji gaped at the dancing flame as though it were an extravagant feast from another world. He reached out and grabbed the match from its lit end, allowing for the invisible tendril to slip away, and then adjusted his grasp to hold the wooden stick. The flame was not snuffed out.

"This is going to be *amazing*," Kenji whispered. He knelt down near a partially completed coloring book—opened to a picture of a forest, scribbled in with crayons of varying shades of gray and black—and held the match to one corner.

OO4

Sitting on the roof in the shade of the stairwell's entrance, I opened *Magical Girl Monthly*.

From what I can tell, the magazine will have one page dedicated to each monster encounter.

Will have? Yes, because all pages that come after the Water Droplets—are redacted.

I have no information on *who* should fight *what,* or *when* and *where* the monsters will appear.

And the magazine won't reveal everything at once—because *that* would be too easy. The second monster page updated itself earlier today—along with the magical girl needed to defeat them. I guess when it gets closer to the time of battle, I'll find out the "where" and "when."

So, every day since Nana's battle, I've flicked through to see if a monster would appear that day.

I have no idea what I'll do if the enemy appears on a weekend, when I won't be able to retrieve the magazine from my desk...

I shook my head.

No, that probably won't happen.

On a lighter note, let me roast the monsters' names.

I mean, Water *Droplets?* That implies something *small*—not the large, gelatinous creatures that absorbed the students on my first day here.

I flipped to the next page: *Fire Flares*. Don't know what *I* would name them, but practically anything is better than *Fire Flares*.

If I ever meet the person who named all of these—even *if* it's Flan Girl—I'm definitely going to sit them down and ask them *what* they were thinking.

Thinking about the monsters' naming conventions makes me wonder why *they* get names, but their domains *don't*. I've searched for any indication in the magazine that the dimension we go to has a name, but came out empty-handed.

Guess *I'll* have to name them.

Great.

To keep it simple, maybe something color-coded? So, the Water Droplets' dimension—if I ever return—will be "the Blue World."

I honestly can't tell if that's more or less original than *Cute, Pretty, Beautiful* calling *their* monsters' dimension "*There*."

If I could, I would've gone through all the other future monsters to silently scoff at their names.

But this was all just a big distraction—the Fire Flares' page updated.

I need to find Youko and get to the library.

Not bothering to stuff the magazine back into my bag, I stood and ran down all the stairs that would take me to the first floor. If there were absolutely no risk of anyone spotting me, I would've transformed and jumped down one stairwell—much faster to skip all the extraneous hallways.

My hopes of getting there before the fire started were crushed—the library was already burning, and the fire was quickly spreading to the adjacent hall.

This fire didn't seem real—almost like an illusion of fancy papers flapping in the air, *fwip fwip fwip,* while lit in cycling colors from below—

But it also seemed to be alive, crawling on the ceiling and licking at the walls, hissing at anyone who approached.

And that would be me.

There was no smoke from where the flames made contact with the school's walls—were they waiting to burn the building down? Staking it out until they decided the best time to strike, like a group of cats stalking their prey?

It gave me the feeling that reaching over to pet them, scratching them behind the ears—if they even *had* any—wouldn't burn my hand.

If they weren't monsters set on destroying the school and potentially taking over the world, I'd be tempted to try it.

Maybe.

Youko walked ahead of me—unaware of the fire, her nose in a book.

The Fire Flares—seemingly more aware of their surroundings than the Water Droplets—aimed a few sparks her book, so as not to be ignored.

The pages ignited, and she finally gave the Fire Flares their desired attention—dropping the book to the ground and covering her mouth in horror.

I ran as fast as I could to catch up to her.

The Flares loomed over her and pounced—wanting to burn more than just paper. Youko tripped and fell to the floor.

She squeezed her eyes shut and waited for the fire to engulf her.

I unrolled *Magical Girl Monthly* and held it aloft with both hands—shielding us from the fire.

Wow.

That actually worked.

"Are you okay?"

Youko opened her eyes after realizing that the heat never came. "I believe so."

I shook out the magazine and inspected it—no soot, and the paper wasn't even curling from the heat.

Youko's gaze was locked on her original destination, and a pained expression crossed her face.

The flames licked at the walls—with the school library at the center of it all.

She squeezed her eyes shut once more, taking in a deep breath and letting it out. When she opened her eyes again, her face was back to its blank slate. "Yes. I'm all right."

"Stop lying." With the Fire Flares temporarily deflected, I pulled

Youko to her feet and flicked to the correct page in *Magical Girl Monthly* and tore out a strip. Youko winced.

"Please, cease your abuse of..." She blinked. "Isn't that the magazine I told you not to bring to school?"

"Yes, it is." I shoved the dark blue paper to her chest—its shades of blue formed waves and bubbles, creating the illusion of motion if you stared at it deeply for too long. "Just take this." Once she took it from me, I turned to face the library doors and extended my arms, opening the portal.

A rift in the fabric of space—Youko gasped.

I ignored her and began my transformation. "I, Takako, take this task of delivering justice to this evil in the form of another hero. Please, let me guide her on her journey to her true destiny—protector of this Earth. I don my mask and responsibility as her mentor. I, Takako, now sleep as I wear this mask—and my true power awakens!"

I *really* need to figure out if I can shorten that...

The strip of paper Youko held to her chest flared out, forming a bow with a brooch at the center. A blue light enveloped her entire body.

"This is..." Once the light faded away, she looked down at her outfit.

She stood before me in different shades and tints of blue: a tiered skirt—the bottom tier being translucent—over a leotard. She wore a sleeveless, cropped vest—very idol-like—with long, mismatched gloves, one dark and one light. Her Hessian boots were mismatched as well, but the opposite colors of her gloves.

"How did you do this? Did you rearrange the atoms of my clothing using—"

I raised a hand to silence her. "It's magic."

She shuddered. "*No.*"

"I have to say—it's weird that this is localized to *just* the school library," I mused, looking up at the flames. "Last time, it had to have been the entire stretch of road outside the school, at *least*. Well, we'll take care of it."

I looked back to Youko. She was pulling at the hem of her skirt, self-consciously.

"Or, I mean...*you'll* take care of it."

"What." It was more of a statement than a question.

"Yeah. You're a magical girl. You have to fight the fire."

"How am I supposed to fight it?" Youko looked down at her blue outfit and extrapolated: *Water will damage the library. I refuse to harm the books.*

"Sometimes, you have to break eggs." I knelt down—barely dodging another spark aimed at my head. Now the only thing I could do was wait for Youko to enter the portal.

She hesitated, looking down at me.

Am I a statue, too realistic for your liking? Get in the portal!

As though she heard my impatient thoughts, Youko stepped through the portal, and I closed it behind her.

OO5

The whole world was on fire, but not all of the flames were monsters. The ground glowed from within—a light moving to different cracks in the embers.

Youko stood in front of me, gloved hands clasped together—almost twiddling her thumbs, though that would still be too much emotion for her.

I looked up. The sky matched the ground. No, it can't be called a sky—it's a ceiling, with no walls for as far as I can see.

How is that even possible?

It was also much more obvious here than in the school—the living flames produced no heat.

We were walking in the heart of a campfire, but not even the ground radiated more than a chill.

A reverse fire? Were the flames absorbing heat instead of emitting it?

Behind Youko, monsters danced the tango, grasping the ceiling as they leapt out of thin fissures.

"Kurosawa. Where are we?"

"We're here."

"But *where* is 'here'?"

That's a good question: Where are we?

Is this the same world as the one that housed the Water Droplets? No idea. It sure doesn't look like it, but with the differences in Earth's climates, anything's possible—the Blue World could be a neighboring area, or a different dimension altogether from this one.

That being said, I guess it really *is* up to me to name it.

I removed my fist from my chin, gesturing at the infinite landscape. "It's the Red World."

Nailed it.

"Then I suppose that this is related to the story of the red *oni* and blue *oni?*"

"Not at all." Too many questions. I gestured to the distance where the Fire Flares swarmed. "Look, can we just get on with the battle?"

"Not until you tell me everything." A light shone in her eyes, reflecting her thirst for knowledge.

Or maybe that was just from the burning world.

Those two things are pretty hard to tell apart.

"Well, in that case..." I faced the oncoming fire. "I'll let you know when I know everything. Sound like a deal?"

Youko hesitated. She looked at the living flames—her face was illuminated by the burning...well, *everything*. Finally, she gulped before nodding. "I will hold you to your word." The ground crackled and steamed under her boots as she walked forward. "Will you at the very least inform me how to produce water to fight them?"

"Hold out your hands," I said, "and *believe.*"

"I believe," Youko replied, and—since the first time I've met her—exclaimed, "in *science!*"

Two torrents of water, one light and one dark, came from her palms, corkscrewing before hitting the nearest Fire Flare.

Its flame dwindled but stayed lit, hissing in our direction.

"Great!" I chimed. "Now, do it maybe, fifty more times? Two hits per monster should do the trick."

She seems to be picking up how to fight monsters faster than Nana—which is strange, considering she's a bookworm. Her most strenuous exercises are those of the mind.

Nana, on the other hand, is an athlete. She has a *six-pack* for crying out loud...unless that's just a modification that comes with her transformation into the magical girl of plants?

Youko sent out another corkscrew of water. "Do you have any other techniques I can use?"

"Hmm..." I thought back to *Magical Girl Monthly*. "Cup your hands like this."

She did as I demonstrated—framing her brooch with her hands, fingers dangling and elbows sticking out. "I do not understand how this will do anything."

"*Believe.*"

Bubbles—no, not bubbles, but wobbling orbs of water—emerged from her brooch and whooshed towards the flames. Unlike the Water Droplets, these didn't seem to be alive.

I reached down to grab the pudding and flan that the Fire Flares left behind, then craned my neck to look up at the ceiling—specifically the crevices.

What's in there?

"Hey, can you aim for that hole?"

Youko looked at me, then to the ceiling where I was pointing. "Why?"

"That's where the flames are coming from," I explained as I stood up straight. "I think..."

We waited for a few seconds, forgetting the superstition that *a watched pot never boils*—or in this case, *a watched crack won't spew flames.*

That probably sounds better in my head. *Really* glad I didn't say that out loud.

"That was a waste of time," Youko stated, facing the flames that were creeping up on her.

As though sensing only one person's attention, two more Fire Flares emerged from the crack. They locked on to Youko's location and immediately flew at her, on the prowl and ready to attack.

"Watch out!"

The words were barely out of my mouth—Youko aimed one torrent of water at them while she kept aiming the other at the creeping flames.

"I have it under control."

As always—I replied with snark.

Once the flames were extinguished, she turned to me with a puzzled look in her eye. "What is that supposed to mean?" Is that an eyebrow raise I see?

"Well, you're so cool-headed—in control of your emotions and stuff," I replied. "I mean, there *were* a few times since the monsters showed up that you weren't, and showed me your more *emotional* side, but—"

"And you will never see that side again." Youko shot a corkscrew of water at the ceiling crack. With enough pressure, the charcoal crumbled.

"And why not?"

Flan and some pudding cups fell from the sky as Youko looked at me, blankly, as though I hadn't just unlocked a hint to her backstory.

"It is none of your concern."

I wanted to press further, but she walked away to find other ceiling crevices that needed the flames inside to be extinguished. "Is this all that I am needed for?" she asked.

"There should be a *giant* fireball somewhere around here. When you defeat that, everything else will disappear—and a door will show up that leads home."

"So unless everything is defeated, there is no way to return?"

"If I find a way, I'll let you know."

After all, isn't *that* a part of knowing everything?

oo6

What was left of the coloring book lay open, pages crinkling and breaking apart, falling onto the pages beneath like dead leaves. Stray matches surrounded the book. Flames slowed their waltz, dwindling. Smoke pooled on the ground like a low, bubbling fog.

Kenji watched, his eyes reflecting the light until he was in the dark once again. He crouched down and silently collected each match, alternating between picking them up from the stick or head, showing no discomfort from the residual heat.

You didn't make them last long—the voice said.

"You didn't tell me that they'd *stop burning*," Kenji complained. He fell from the balls of his feet to his rear and crossed his legs.

"You must get used to the fleeting existence of material objects. Everything is temporary—a rule of the universe that we will soon be enforcing."

"But *why?*" Kenji pouted. "And if everything's temporary, doesn't that mean the Darkness—"

"When nothing exists, there will only be the Darkness. The absence of light, the absence of stars... The night sky will be consumed by the pure Darkness—for us to observe. The humans show no appreciation for the Darkness, and so we must teach them that nothing they have created will last."

"If we're gonna be the ones to 'force the rules, we can make them whatever we want," Kenji mumbled. His eyes had glazed over halfway through the speech. "And I want things to burn. *Forever.*"

"Flames give off many things—light. Heat. Chemicals. The illusion of control—but they are a force to be reckoned with. The Darkness is our dominion. We came from it, so we can control it."

Kenji cupped his hands together and squeezed the used matches tightly, the wood poking at his skin. After a moment, he asked: *Why are they wet?*

"It's natural for items to become wet if you bleed on them," the voice explained.

"But I'm not bleeding!" Kenji uncurled his fingers. "They were wet when I picked them up!" He dropped the used matches, but they didn't reach his lap, instead disappearing into the void. Ignoring this, he looked at his hands, then held them out upturned for the voice to observe.

His palms were the canvas for a morbid sketch—uneven, black shapes spread out from where his hands met, swirling out to his fingers and wrists.

"Wipe that away right now. It is unbecoming of you."

"But it looks like you, Father!"

OO7

"Will the library be all right when we return?"

"When the Water Droplets were defeated, there was a downpour."

"Water Droplets?"

"*So,*" I continued, ignoring her, "there *is* going to be some sort of *equivalent event* to replace everyone else's memories of the monsters."

Her shoulders fell.

"I mean, it'll *probably* be a fire drill or something minor." I waved my hands about, floundering as I tried to reassure her: *I don't think the entire library will be gone.*

Youko stepped through the red door—and we were back at school.

I rubbed my eyes. The hallway felt too dim after looking at all that fire. Unlike Nana, Youko made no attempt to help me up—she backed away from the library, tripping over me as I stood.

"Whoa, careful!" I said, steadying her.

"The books..."

"What? There's no fire, no scorch marks—no damage at all!" Though as I said this, a hint of burnt paper reached my nose.

Youko choked on a gasp, covering her mouth to prevent the escape of any more emotion.

So much for you hiding that side of yourself from me...

"That...really could be anything?" Though with the scent of burning paper in a library, there aren't many options for what it *could* be.

"No. There is nothing else it could be," Youko insisted, once again monotone.

Gee, I'm trying to be reassuring here.

Holding onto one of her arms to make sure she didn't run off or collapse, I reached for the library door, wanting to prove her wrong.

The door pushed into my hand as someone exited in a rush.

Coughing.

"What happened?" I asked.

"F—" Hotaru coughed. "*Fire!*"

Another whiff of burnt paper wafted out, accompanied by some smoke.

If there *was* a fire—it was very small, or already extinguished.

Back against the wall, Hotaru slid to the floor and coughed one more time. She muttered something about the bad luck of being seventeen—about how her life seemed to be perfectly normal when she was sixteen.

Dropping off Youko and all of my critical thinking skills at the door, I stepped into the library and followed the burning stench.

A trash can next to a study table appeared to be the source. Once full of discarded paper, there was now nothing but ash. A light flashed in the corner of my eye—a magnifying glass on a shelf near a window.

Now, I don't know anything about the science of lighting paper on fire with a magnifying glass and the sun—what angles are involved in getting the temperature right.

However.

I *do* know that being in the wrong place at the wrong time *could* get me accused of—and arrested for—*arson*. So, I retraced my steps quickly, while trying not to look suspicious.

I was barely out the door when Youko asked, *Is there a fire?*

"There was, but it burned itself out. Nothing's damaged except for some scrap paper."

Youko closed her eyes, hand over her heart in relief—but then retracted this, realizing Hotaru was also present.

Wait. Should we be outside right now? The fire alarm's not going off, but...

Without saying another word, Youko walked over to her shoe locker and changed from her *uwabaki* to her loafers to head outside.

I guess we're not talking about anything that just happened.

Okay.

I went to follow Youko—and she collapsed against the lockers.

Time seemed to slow down as Hotaru rushed past me, scrambling across the floor, practically crawling. She slid to a halt like a batter into home, breaking Youko's fall.

"Sa-fe!" Hotaru said, her voice a hushed cheer, before lying down, exhausted.

I sprinted over. "So, should we take her to the infirmary? Or is everyone outside because of the fire?"

"Hell if *I* know," Hotaru replied. She slung Youko's arm over her shoulders as she stood. "I had my earbuds in." Youko's head lolled about as Hotaru shrugged her shoulder. "Don't let her know, 'kay? The *vigilante* will confiscate my phone."

Vigilante? Does she know about us being magical girls?

Always getting into everyone's business even though she has no real authority—Hotaru ranted. "Kinda annoying, y'know?"

Ah. "Yeah, but I don't really know the school rules yet, so having Youko tell me is actually helpful. It's better *she* tells me if I'm doing something wrong before a teacher does and I get disciplined for it."

"Ha, well don't let her know you haven't read the handbook. She'll have a *fit!*"

We were only a few steps away from the main entrance, shoe change be damned—when a chipper voice behind us asked: *A kidnapping?*

I turned around and saw Tsubasa. I looked at Hotaru and Youko's compromising position, then back to Tsubasa.

"No! Youko just needs some fresh air!" I explained.

Tsubasa examined the situation a bit more, eyes widening.

"You dummies!" She stamped her foot.

Wow, I'm honestly taken aback! How could you *say* that?

"If Youko has a fainting spell, you have to take her to the infirmary!"

"Ah, you're right," Hotaru said. She hoisted Youko onto her back and sped to the infirmary, right around the corner.

"But..." I waved my hands. "Isn't everybody outside for the fire?"

Tsubasa tilted her head to the side. "What fire?"

Crap. If the fire alarm didn't go off after all, that means that no one knows about the library fire. Because *I* was the first to mention it, that puts me at the top of the list of suspects. Hotaru and Youko would be suspects, too.

"There's a fire outside?" she asked, walking to the school's entrance.

Ah. You misunderstood the location.

She looked out the windows. "Where?"

Well, at least I'll be able to successfully distract her from what I said about a fire by giving her my flan cup at lunch tomorrow.

"Whoa!" She pressed her cheek against the glass to get as good a view she could without opening the door and stepping out.

I scowled. "What's 'whoa'?"

"There're scorch marks in the grass! How'd *that* happen?"

Sure enough, there were patches of dead grass here and there. To me, though, it looked sunburned—not caused by the Fire Flares. Though that could be part of the cover-up this time around, like the Water Droplets' rain?

"I—"

Tsubasa let out a gasp and stamped her foot once more. "The aliens came and didn't even say hi to me!"

What.

oo8

"Suzu!" Noriko exclaimed. She knelt down and held the unconscious girl upright, patting her gently on the cheek in an attempt to wake her. Jet and Bone, back in their rabbit forms, rushed to the girls' side.

"You *idiots*." Atsuko stepped forward. "If Suzu has a fainting spell, you have to take her to the hospital! It's not something you can just *wish away* like the rest of our pain!"

That sounds familiar. Does Tsubasa watch this show, too?
And *the rest of our pain?* When did this show get so *dark?*
Wait, am I actually getting invested in it?

"We're doing what's best for her," Bone insisted.
"How do *you* know what's best for her?" Atsuko screamed, falling to her knees.
"It's our best *judgment!*" Bone shrieked, hair spiking up like a cat's.

Does he have sharp teeth all the time?

Noriko's eyes widened in shock at the sudden outburst.
Jet turned away from everyone.
"I just don't know who I should believe anymore," Noriko whispered, leaning over Suzu, shaking as she started to cry.
"Believe *me,*" Atsuko said, kneeling down next to her two friends and the Elves.

"Our powers as Goddesses can only do so much. Same with Jet and Bone. None of us can cure Suzu, but the hospital can fix her up. And—no offense, guys," she said, turning to the Elves, "but when you offered to extend her life before, that wasn't *life*."

Did I miss an episode?

Oh no. I *am* invested.

I took out my phone and looked up a fan page summarizing each episode to confirm—no, this is just a rerun of the third episode before the fourth one airs.

So that line can only be referring to something from last season.

I started a search for the previous season—the same title, but without *Heart-Throbbing Season* tacked on the end.

Aside from a promotional image or two, and some out-of-context screenshots that reveal none of the story...

Nothing.

Nowhere to watch it, nowhere to buy it, and no plot summaries.

I looked up and saw that Suzu was now awake. What had happened when I was looking down? Did Jet and Bone heal her?

The camera zoomed out from above the scene, and the episode was over.

Of course, I hadn't been obsessed over this show last week, and zoned out during the credits. I walked up to the TV and turned the volume up.

It was a melancholic song, starting out with piano before getting fleshed out with strings and other instruments.

Was this used in the second episode? I know the first one used the opening credits at the end, but this...

This seems *too* sad, even though the series seems to be darker than it originally let on.

A single image panned up from the bottom of the screen. Someone was lying in a bed full of flowers. Pitch-black hands reached out from the petals to her white dress and out towards the audience.

The camera panned down further, revealing a single white rose on her stomach. She clasped her hands together, tightly, almost in prayer.

Finally, the camera revealed her face. It was Gorgeous, the Deadly Omen Finder. With her eyes closed, her expression was peaceful—not at all bored or evil as in her debut appearance this season. Her hair flowed out around her as though she was floating in a river.

The screen faded to black, showing my reflection as I waited for the next episode to start, and hopefully explain what just happened.

In true anime fashion, my wish was fulfilled in the form of a cold open.

Noriko continued to cry over Suzu's body. One *special* tear glowed with golden glitter over a black background to emphasize how *special* it really was, in case the viewer couldn't tell.

The tear fell on Suzu's cheek, and she stirred.

Noriko pulled away slightly, to make sure she wasn't imagining the movement.

The purple-haired girl slowly opened her eyes, tilting her head to look around the best she could. "What happened?"

Noriko's tears fell faster, and Atsuko joined her in crying viscous tears, tightly hugging Suzu.

After the opening credits, Jet hopped over to Noriko's side, placing a paw on her thigh.

"Your powers as a Goddess have given her life."

"My powers?"

"With your Angelic Goddess powers, you control light and life. You're able to heal anyone with your tears."

Like how *I* use *pudding?*

Bone's ears flicked backwards. "Watch out!" he yelled, turning into his true Elf form and shielding everyone with light from an oncoming barrage of scrap metal spears.

"I sensed an Omen," Gorgeous droned. "*Hilarious* that it's the three of you, with your *pets* that I find here instead."

Jet growled at her. She snarled back.

"*Anyway*," Gorgeous continued, reaching out her hand for Suzu, "you're coming with me. Now."

Suzu lifted her hand, but hesitated.

"*What?!*" Noriko and Atsuko cried out in unison.

"You can't be *serious* about going with her, Suzu!" Atsuko exclaimed.

"Yeah!" Noriko agreed. "She's sided with the Deadly Omen Finders!"

"She doesn't have a choice," Gorgeous stated. "Because *you* 'healed' her, she'll turn into an Omen at any moment."

"You're wrong!" Bone exclaimed, getting to his feet. "You just wanna extract Pretty's Angelic Goddess powers from Cute to create Omens that can't be defeated!"

"Hm." Gorgeous paused for a second, crossing her arms and bringing one index finger to her lips, contemplating this. "You're partially right. Close enough."

An unseen force lifted Suzu out of her friends' arms, carrying her kicking and screaming to the top of a lamp post—where she melted into an orb that appeared out of nothing.

"Suzu!"

"I'll be taking my leave now," Gorgeous said, tipping her small hat. She spun on her heel, coattails fluttering in the breeze.

"No you don't!" Bone shouted, trying to reach her.

"You're the most *useless* Elf," Gorgeous replied, jumping to the same lamp post as she summoned her spears, along with street signs uprooted from the surrounding area.

"*Bone!*"

The screen flashed to show a black silhouette over a red background, right before impact.

I winced.
This is going to *hurt*.

A close up of Bone's iris, pulsing in horror.

"Atsu..." Her name was lost in his throat.

Bone sat on the ground, unharmed, having been pushed out of the way in the nick of time.

Atsuko lay on the ground, unmoving, impaled from multiple directions by the shrapnel—censored for television by dark shadows where the metal intersected her body.

I jolted at the reveal, instinctively reaching for my neck.
Well, *that* was unexpected.

Gorgeous ignored the cries of those she once considered friends as she disappeared in a cloud of smoke.

With a cut to commercials, I realized I'd been holding my breath with my palm still resting on my throat.

I coughed.

"I guess I should take a cough drop."

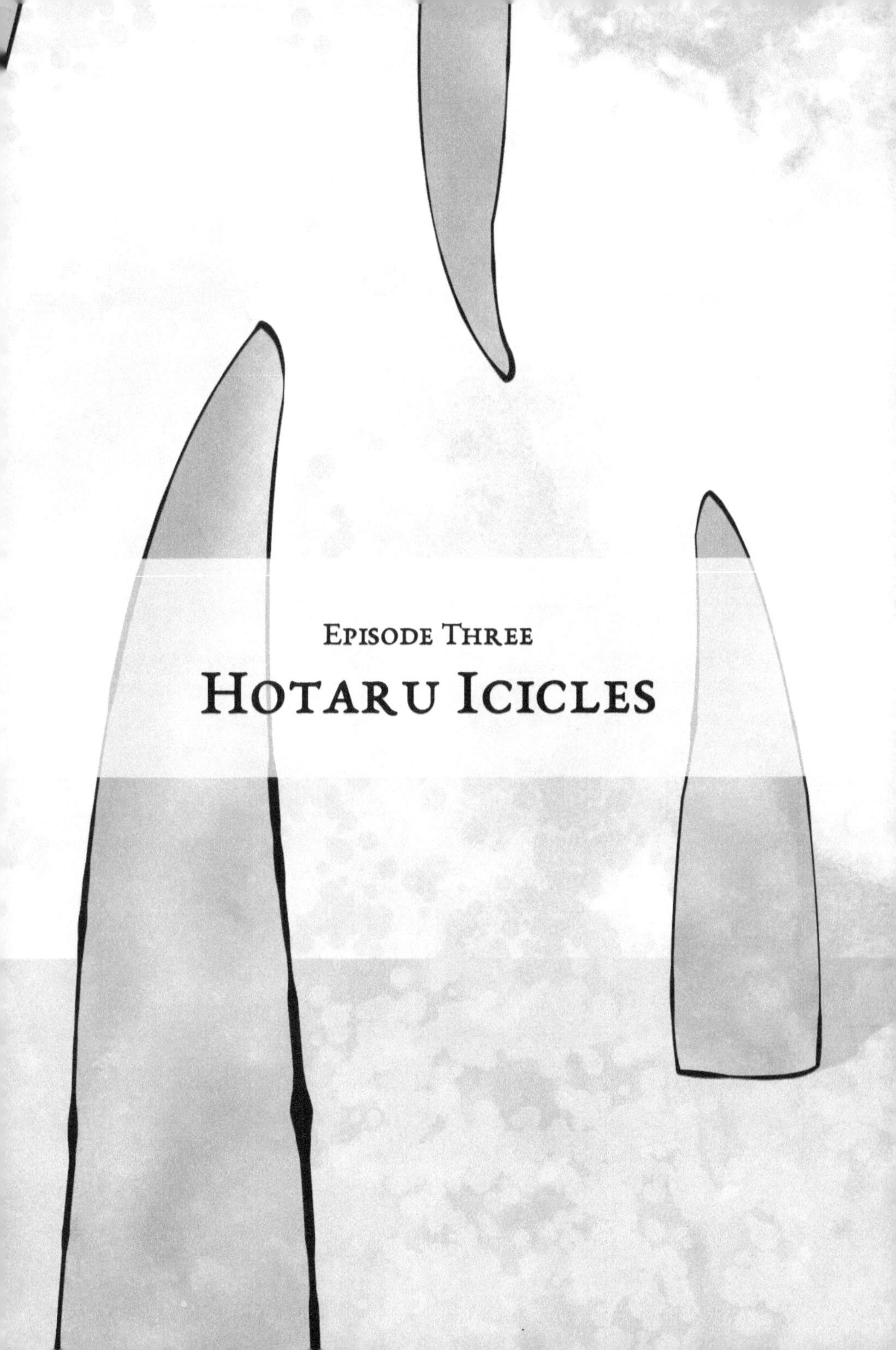

Episode Three
Hotaru Icicles

OOI

QUESTION: What is your opinion on Fujioka High School's seventh mystery—*magical girls?*

SAITO WAKANA: No comment.

Really? Everyone has at least *some* opinion of them!

SAITO: Masuyo. *Please* stop talking to me.

Wakana stared at the recorder before flicking its switch and continuing to pack her bag.

"Oh, *fine.*" The interviewer pouted, adjusting their braid before turning their attention to me. "Heyyy! I don't think we've talked before!"

"Yeah," I replied, taking one last bite from my lunch—a pork cutlet sandwich.

I had given Tsubasa my flan—*out of the blue* as she had put it—and now I regretted not bringing another cup for myself. It makes for a great distraction from socializing.

"Yamauchi Masuyo!" the interviewer announced, giving me a relaxed salute. Why? Why a salute? "It's a pleasure."

I looked down at their reporter's notepad. "So, are you in the Newspaper Club or something?"

Or something—Wakana sighed. She stood up, adjusting the purple bow pinned to her long, silver hair, and left the classroom.

The purple-haired girl who sat closest to the back door—Watanabe Tomoko—followed after an exaggerated pause that, to anyone not paying attention, would look natural.

I, of course, had been paying attention on a daily basis in case one of them needs to transform.

I turned to face Masuyo, who was now inches away from my face.

Soooo, I'm Yamauchi Masuyo, they reiterated. "President of the Paranormal Club! I'm researching the sudden appearance of *magical girls* as part of Fujioka High School's Seven Mysteries!"

"Magical girls, huh? That doesn't seem very *paranormal* to me..."

"There's *magic* in the *name!*" Masuyo exclaimed. "The *source* of their power could be supernatural! They could be reincarnations of *aliens!* Or—ooh, wouldn't *this* be cool?—they could have gotten their powers by selling their souls to a *demon!* Or *maybe* their powers are angelic in nature! But my *favorite* theory so far just *has* to be that there was a ritual performed by a *cult,* and—"

"Yeah, I don't think so." I closed the lid of my *bento.*

"Aw, come on! Anything's possible, right?"

"Depends, I guess. Besides, what gives you the authority to claim these magical girls as the school's?"

"All major news sources—and some minor—have brought up Fujioka High School as the backdrop to these magical girl battles! It's only fair that *we* claim them as our own!"

So, Takako—what's *your* opinion on the magical girl situation?

KUROSAWA TAKAKO: The same as everyone else. It's probably an ad campaign. A publicity stunt. Maybe for that one magical girl anime.

Not *everyone* thinks that, so don't put words in their mouths. I've collected all those theories I mentioned before from our classmates! Something's *off* about it all. Like how did they pull off all those stunts? The plants? The water?

92

KUROSAWA: Trained acrobats. Wires. Smoke and mirrors. A hose.

But what about the fact that no one *remembers* the monsters appearing, and that only two videos *total* have surfaced—one for each girl?

KUROSAWA: Publicity. Stunt.

"Aw, you're no *fun...*" Masuyo pouted and closed their notepad.

I sighed slightly in relief as Masuyo walked back to their seat, and pictured a more truthful answer to the question posed: *Or maybe it's actual magic. Because sure—why not? I mean, that's my best guess.*

I keep getting asked questions I don't know the answers to...

Maybe I should start asking questions of my own?

Like, who put *Magical Girl Monthly* in my desk? Was it Flan Girl? Why can't the magazine leave the school?

Who keeps my fridge stocked at home?

Why can't I remember anything from before I woke up on the sofa?

I looked over to Youko's seat. She hadn't attended school since her battle—maybe she was feeling more exhausted than Nana due to her pre-existing condition?

Why did they have different reactions after their transformations reverted? It seemed that Nana was the most worn out the day of the library fire—so will Youko be at her worst the day of the next battle?

I sighed and stood up, casually sliding *Magical Girl Monthly* into my bag.

There's still time left in the break, so why not go to the roof?

OO2

The roof had very quickly earned its place as my favorite spot at school. It's not that I don't have a fear of heights—the idea of leaning over the balcony too far is an ever-present weight in my stomach—but the roof is serene.

Ah, yes. The roof. Devoid of anyone else most of the time—is there a rule that says we shouldn't be up here?

Oh well.

Regardless—I can look at the sky and feel the breeze and be left to my own thoughts as they take shape in the clouds.

Today, however, was not one of those days.

Today, my entrance consisted of almost hitting two of my classmates with the door.

"*Watch* it."

"Oh. Sorry," I replied.

Wakana looked down her nose at me with her cold, violet eyes. "Let's go, Tomoko." She pushed past me, and Tomoko followed.

I tried unjamming the door from its open position, but it just *refused* to swing shut.

After a few grunts, I turned my head slightly. Tomoko had paused on the stairwell to watch me.

"What?" I asked.

Pull up and in—she stated, before leaving me to mull it over.

After managing to close the door—on my first attempt after Tomoko's advice—I walked over to my usual spot and sat down in the shade created by the stairs' enclosure.

I took the magazine and a notebook out of my bag.

Its cover had changed at the start of May—and I was no longer the cover girl.

Instead, Nana stood in her magical girl attire with a wide smile, one fist on her hip, the other by her head as she flexed her exposed bicep.

Yeah.

She did *not* pose for this picture.

The cover was the only change to the magazine—the magical girl profiles and existing monster pages remained the same.

Without further ado, I opened my notebook and started writing as fast as my hand could keep up with my train of thought.

This was easy until the train was no longer in the station—and my hand was waiting on the platform for the next arrival.

I balanced my pencil on my pursed lips like a mustache, reading over what I had written.

Well, at least I started asking questions. But there're just so many that I can't get them in the right order...

The first few questions had been my train of thought back in the classroom, but after that they started to go all over the place.

I tried drawing lines to connect them, but going over the page multiple times in one only color—silver pencil lead—made things more confusing.

Why doesn't anyone remember the monsters? Hotaru had gotten caught in a Water Droplet, but now thought that she'd been caught in the rain.

Who had filmed Nana's battle? I'll have to ask someone later to see the video of Youko's battle...but it's probably the same as Nana's—monsters attacking people outside the school.

Why can't anyone remember being recorded?

What happens if someone tries to talk to the battling magical girl?

I leaned against the wall and sneezed, causing the pencil to fall from my lip.

"Why does this have to be so *hard?*"

The wind flipped the pages of the magazine and my notebook. I fiddled lazily with one of the zippers on my bag.

There's nothing that I can *find* in the magazine that says I *can't* tell everyone about everyone else's secret identities—but like Masuyo said, something about it still feels off.

Any time I even *think* about revealing to the class that I'm the one behind the magical girls, I feel a tightening in my throat. Strange enough, it's not anxiety—I'm pretty confident that I know how my anxiety response feels.

Instead, this feels like a weight—a *magical* weight—that has the express purpose to prevent me from revealing anything before it's necessary. It only goes away when I give up my hope of sharing excessive information.

I closed my eyes and sighed, wishing I could just stay up here for the rest of the day instead of going back to class.

OO3

Wakana and Tomoko stared at me as I returned to the classroom from my brainstorming session.

They must have been talking about me.

I settled back into my seat, and they continued to stare at me as the final magical-girl-to-be approached me.

About *time*.

I was beginning to wonder if *I'd* have to initiate a conversation with *her*.

"Hi. I'm Abe Miku." The teal-haired girl's hand twitched at her side, as though she wanted to offer her hand for me to shake, but was too nervous to do so. She settled for reaching up quickly to adjust her glasses, before her hand fell back down to hang at her side.

"And I'm Kurosawa Takako." I blinked in waiting.

Is she going to ask to copy my homework or something?

Or is she going to talk to me about magical girls, too?

"Do you want to be friends?"

"Uh..." Not what I was expecting.

Is she the first of my classmates to ask me that directly? Does Tsubasa see me as a friend? Does anyone else? At what point in knowing someone do you silently acknowledge that you're friends instead of casual acquaintances?

"Sure."

Miku beamed, though her smile couldn't hide a look of relief in her eyes. Was she expecting me to reply with, *Sorry, I already have too many friends* or something? She adjusted her glasses once again, and merely stood there.

I couldn't think of anything else to say, and filling the air with a random tongue twister is Nana's gimmick. "So…"

Miku blinked. "Hm?"

Well, I can always fall back on *that* topic…

I shifted in my seat. "How 'bout those magical girls?"

"Earth and water going up against water and fire…" Miku mused. "I mean, what *is* this? An RPG?"

"Yeah. I know, right?"

"My prediction is that the next one will have control over *air,* and then a final girl will have power over *fire.* To balance everything out, you know? There's no *need* to have more than four magical girls in one city—or, heck, one *school.*"

"But why four?"

"It's an even number." Miku adjusted her glasses once more. "Then again, the number four *is* unlucky—and teams of five *are* traditional in the genre. I shouldn't let my personal preference get in the way of *tradition.*"

"Oh." There's gonna be *way* more than five.

Miku turned Tsubasa's chair around and sat down like she was joining me at a tiny café table. Her knees briefly bumped against mine, but she scooted the chair back so we both had enough foot room.

And then, she began her rant.

"Okay, so I *know* that these aren't *real* magical girls. *There's no such thing,* yeah yeah—but it would be cool if they *were* real. Maybe not *magic,* but advanced *science* that *looks* like magic, but—I'm getting ahead of myself. *Anyway…*" Miku tapped her fingers on my desk. "It's easier to divide the area of the city into four. Four magical girls can patrol those four corners every night, yeah?"

"Doesn't the city have *more* than four corners?"

"Yes, yes it does—but we're going to ignore that small bit of information to focus on this idea." Miku tapped her finger on my desk four times, making a square with the points.

Okay.

"Obviously, we can't tell if there's a pattern yet with when the monsters will show up from just two appearances," Miku explained. "It's not enough data to determine when the next one will appear, if there's a pattern at all. In terms of *where* they appear," she laughed, "you could say that they *may* be centralized around our school. I mean, if I recall correctly, the earth magical girl appeared on your first day. With the existing data, I could say that *you* have something to do with all of this. But as you know," she said in sing-song, "*correlation doesn't equal causation* and all that!"

I tried suppressing a gulp. My anxiety towards being discovered probably came off as fear when I asked, "So, there's no pattern with the times the monsters appear?"

"Can't say right now. I mean, yeah, they appeared towards the end of the school day. *But* they weren't on the same day of the week. Tuesday, April twentieth. Wednesday, April twenty-eighth. A week after one another—"

"Are you saying the next one's going to be today?"

Miku crossed her arms and pursed her lips. "Ah, that's right. It *is* Thursday the sixth, isn't it..." She shook her head dismissively and shrugged. "It's really hard to say based on just the two. I mean, what if these aren't the only battles that've been going on? What if they're the only battles that've been witnessed by the *public?*"

"Huh?"

"Every day—starting off who really *knows* when?—magical girls might've been fighting monsters. It's only when things get *really* out of hand—that the monsters come into town—that we see them."

"Are you saying they're not doing their jobs right?"

Miku blinked, fidgeting nervously.

"Are you thinking that they'll come to you if they somehow hear what you said and interpret it as a personal attack?"

"Uh..." She regained her composure almost immediately. "They're doing just fine. It's just...I guess it's like when your grade drops from forgetting your homework at home? Magical girls are human, too...probably."

"Probably?"

"Yeah, Masuyo talked to you about this before, right? The magical girls could be *ethereal* or something, and that's how they transform. Or maybe they started out as human, but their transformations are making them less so?"

Wow. *Wow.* I hope not.

We sat in silence, not sure of how to continue from there. Miku stood and walked away awkwardly when she had nothing else to say on the matter, and I couldn't think of another icebreaker.

OO4

"What are you doing with that *contraption?*" The contraption in question—a snow cone machine.

"I dunno," Kenji replied, engrossed by his new toy. "*Miyako* gave it to me." He turned a crank, crushing a questionable material through a hole and into the cup waiting below.

"Where *is* that girl? She should understand that you have no need for this as a being of the Darkness. After I find out how she managed to smuggle it into our domain—I will have it destroyed."

"*No!*" Kenji shouted, taking the cup and hurling its contents into the distance, in the assumed direction of the voice's source.

"Aw, *c'mon!* Don't take it away from him, old man!" Another voice enters the scene—sharp and high-pitched, grating on the ears to the extent that it seemed its owner wanted to elicit annoyed reactions on purpose.

Her family, however, was far too used to it by now.

"We have no need for nutrients, Miyako."

"I know we don't *need* that stuff!" Miyako replied. "So I checked! This doesn't have any of that *healthy* crap! No nutrients—at *all!* It's unhealthy, and the more stuff ya add to it, the worse it is! The sugars will probably eat away at his insides, and he'll end up sacrificing his body to the Darkness faster than you did, old man!"

Probably won't get the same powers as you, though—she clarified.

Their father let out a pained sigh. "Regardless, this machine will corrupt him—have him *crave* more physical objects from the human world."

Kenji sat back down and added more chunks of "ice" to the top of the machine—the chunks that he threw had reset their position to be back at his side. "I'm keeping it no matter what you say, Father."

There was a pause in the conversation, as though Kenji's father was waiting for his son to relent—to give up his shiny, new toy.

The silence was broken by a weary sigh. "I will make an exception this *once*—"

Miyako snorted. "Like with the matches?" There was an audible smirk in her voice.

"—but that does *not* reflect the will of the Darkness. If you continue to make requests such as this, the Darkness will not be as lenient in the future when you really need something, and I will not make a case for you."

"Yes, Father!" Kenji said, agreeing with his words even though he hadn't heard most of them over the "ice" being crushed.

"Remember your roots, Kenji. You came from the Darkness. When you die, you will return to the Darkness. It will judge you on your actions, and if it deems you worthy, it will bring you back. If not, you will be gone from existence forever."

"*Okay,* Father!" Kenji answered, bristling. He removed the cup from below the machine. It contained a small white mountain of "ice," almost flowing over the brim.

After a pause to make sure their father had left, Miyako asked, "So, I *know* I didn't bring ya ice for that. Just the machine and juice or whatever. And some cups. The Darkness only lets me be *so generous.* So, whatcha usin'?"

Teeth, Kenji said—not looking up from his work of squeezing a thick, black sludge over the cup's contents.

"You really *are* my brother!" Miyako cheered.

Kenji looked up in the direction of her voice, smiling—showing off his new set of teeth to her, shinier and leaning more into fang territory.

104

"I'm so proud of you!"

OO5

I stood outside my classroom, back against the wall, looking blankly at the computer lab's windows. There were no stray monitors lit up—I could alternate from looking through to the windows on the far side of the room and my own reflection.

I pondered what *exactly* my life choices could be that led to my memory loss, in *addition* to taking orders from a *stupid* magazine.

Upon looking through it once more during class, I ended up finding the fine print: *Don't let them know about the others*. I guess that explains the tightness in my throat.

They're best friends—so would it *really* be that bad for Nana to find out about Hotaru becoming a magical girl?

Why *do* I need to keep this a secret with *every* magical girl?

Why can't I tell everyone who's in *Magical Girl Monthly* that, "Oh, hey, half of our class is made up of magical girls! Let's have a *magical girl sleepover* where we braid each other's hair and talk about *boys* or whatever. Sure hope a *monster* doesn't show up for the *fourteen of you* to attack!"

Then again, *Magical Girl Monthly* has a lot of information that has yet to be proved wrong.

Maybe if Hotaru and Nana—or any other pairing of besties—realize they're both magical girls, one of them will want to help the other in her time of need?

One could go on the battlefield and get hurt because she wasn't transformed.

No, that's unlikely—we go to the other world, and no one can follow.

Maybe they'd talk to each other about magical girl things.

Someone could overhear...

The force responsible for sending the monsters could overhear, and...

It's a liability.

But you'd think that would be in bold, not hidden among other information.

Though I guess my physical inability to blab helps with that.

Anyway, I have to make Nana leave, or get Hotaru to come out into the hall with me.

Hail tapped against the computer lab's windows before turning into snow, coming down hard enough that I could see it from where I stood. I leaned around the corner to peer into the classroom to see if my two classmates had noticed the drastic change in weather yet.

"What. The. Hell." Hotaru dropped her cleaning rag and pressed her nose and palms to the window.

"You're gonna smudge the glass!"

"Nana." Hotaru grabbed her friend's shoulder, stopping her mid-sweep. "It. Is. *Snowing*."

"Huh?"

"It. Is. *May*."

"Yeah, *early* May. We've still got that April weather happening."

"Just *look!* It shouldn't be snowing this hard, *right?*" Hotaru dragged her friend over to the window.

"Huh." Nana crossed her arms, gathering her thoughts.

"'Huh'? That's all?"

"A snowplow is plowing through the snow."

"Where?" Hotaru asked, squinting out the window.

"Oh, there's no plow..." Nana looked down sheepishly as she poked her index fingers together.

"Ah, a tongue twister. You were just being *you*."

"Well!" Nana chimed. "There's no use staying cooped up in here!" She slid open a window. "Fresh air!"

"Hey, hey, hey! *Fingerprints!* I just cleaned that!"

Nana gave a dismissive hand wave. "And *you* fogged it up by *breathin'* on it. You can wipe it down again!"

"Yeah, yeah..."

Nana gripped the windowsill and leaned out. "Haaaaaah!" she breathed—before pulling her head back in, so quickly she tripped over a chair and fell on her butt on the floor. "Wait, that's...that *can't* be right..."

"What're you going on about?" Hotaru looked down at Nana, who paled like she just saw a ghost.

It's not snow—Nana whispered. She turned to Hotaru and repeated, "It's. *Not. Snow!*"

"Really?" Hotaru snorted and reached for the top of Nana's head, but the green-haired girl pulled away. "What? You've got a little in your hair. Was just gonna get it for you."

Nana quickly stood, bent over, and carded her fingers through her hair—shaking out the not-snow like it was dandruff.

"Jeez, now you gotta sweep again."

Nana grabbed Hotaru's wrist and started walking. "We have to leave. Right. Now."

"Wow, okay. Let go of me, though. You're hurting me."

"Oh, sorry." Nana jerked her hand forward, still gripping Hotaru's.

"I said let *go!*"

"I'm *trying!*"

I slammed the sliding door open, so hard that it practically went off the track. "Nana! Hotaru!" They turned to face me.

Nana looked at me, knowingly. Her hand was in a death grip around Hotaru's wrist, albeit against her will—it was encrusted with a layer of crystal.

"Takako!" Nana called out. "You wouldn't happen to have an ice pick, would you? Ha ha..."

A gust of wind brought more of the not-snow in through the window—it was warm, like the May day that it was.

"Don't let it touch you!" Nana shrieked. She spun, yanking Hotaru behind her.

After selflessly volunteering herself as a shield, the magical girl of plants was out of commission—a frost-bitten head of lettuce with dark, lifeless eyes.

Well, like how that Water Droplet absorbed Hotaru, I'm guessing Nana won't remember this when the monsters are defeated.

Probably.

Hopefully?

"Takako, we have to get out of here!" Hotaru crouched, wrapping her other arm around Nana's waist in a tight hug in an attempt to lift her. "Please, help me carry—"

"She's frozen to the ground, Hotaru," I interjected.

"Yeah, so I need you to help me! Kick the ice on the floor so we can break her free!"

"Don't touch her with your other hand," I continued. "I need you to transform."

"Transform?" she asked, releasing her friend from the awkward hug and standing up.

I removed *Magical Girl Monthly* from my bag, and—sure enough—the next monster's page had updated its arrival time to *right now*.

"Say...were there any Icicles outside the window?"

Hotaru shrugged. "We noticed it was snowing, and Nana stuck her head out. But then she freaked out, saying it wasn't snow?"

So, Nana must have realized it was the work of another monster.

"Have *you* realized it, then?" I asked.

"Hah?" she replied, flatly.

"The window is wide open, and yet it still feels warm. Don't you think if it *were* snowing, it'd be cold inside by now?"

"Nana's *hand* is cold." She looked to her friend, encased in ice. "Well...I guess *more than* her hand is, anyway." She clenched her eyes shut, tossed her head back, and whined, "I'm probably gonna freeze next 'cause she's touching me! Why's my luck so bad?"

I gave my speech as I walked towards her, transforming mid-stride. "I, Takako, take this task of delivering justice to this evil in the form of another hero. Please, let me guide her on her journey to her true destiny, protector of this Earth. I don my mask and responsibility as her mentor.

I, Takako, now sleep as I wear this mask and my true power awakens!"

Hotaru blinked, then rubbed her eyes with her free hand. "What."

I held out my hands, strip of paper in my upturned palms. It was mostly orange—but it didn't look like flames. Instead, the paper had dark lines crisscrossing throughout the design, making it look like embers in a fire. "Your luck is going to change."

"Uh...no offense, Takako..." Hotaru hesitated, looking to me, then the paper, then back at me. "This is a *bit* too much for me to process. I think I'd rather take my chances turning into an ice sculpture."

I extended my hands a bit further.

Take the paper—I said through an insistent smile.

"F-Fine!" She grabbed it from me and shook it around, exasperated. "*Happy* now? I did what you said!" She placed her fist on her hip. "How is this gonna *help* with *anything?*"

The strip of paper slithered out of Hotaru's grasp, snaking around her waist, stretching so much it became thin like twine. Sections of the belt puffed out, making it look like a garland of marshmallows. She closed her eyes as the belt emanated a red light.

"Open your eyes."

Hotaru's school uniform was gone, replaced by a red bodysuit with an orange flame on her stomach going up to her chest. The bodysuit covered her throat, and even went up further to cover her ears. Slits in the fabric exposed her freckled shoulders. Long sleeves continued down her arms and transitioned into gloves. Over the bodysuit was a pair of shorts, a darker red. The belt of marshmallows—some sort of fire starter—had a trail of fabric in the back resembling flames. Her boots were not unlike those of a fire fighter's. Orange baubles adorned her ponytail, and her hair looked like a fire licking the air.

The strong heat radiating passively from Hotaru thawed Nana's frozen grip, just enough for her to slide out. She held her wrist and flexed it, relief spreading on her face when it let out an audible *crack*.

"So, are you gonna transform her, too?"

I blinked.

Had Nana already told her the secret?

Why would *she* get to be exempt from the magazine's rule?

"I mean, we're partners in crime in school, so it'd be *epic* if we could be a magical girl *duo!*"

Well, she doesn't know. That's good.

I opened my mouth, finger in the air as I tried to think of the most eloquent explanation, settling for pointing at Hotaru and saying: *No.*

Hotaru crossed her arms and cocked her hip to the side, then leaned forward. "C'mon, Takako!"

"Hotaru, *no.*"

"Hotaru, *yes!*"

Realizing this was just going to be a back and forth of me saying *no* and her insisting over and over again, I sighed and opened up the portal, crouching down as my consciousness traveled to the other world.

This time, the world was white and shining—a winter wasteland without any of the chill that usually comes with the season.

Icicles—too high up for me to judge their size—glided along the ceiling like ice cubes on a linoleum floor, not aware of my presence yet.

I decided to look through the portal that led back to the classroom, since I had never gotten the chance before.

From this perspective, it wasn't a tear in space—it was an open door, not unlike the exit door that appears at the end of the battles.

Seeing my vacant body was *definitely* strange—as though I had just found a long-lost twin of mine.

Hotaru focused on my body—probably wondering if the not-ice got to me. She made a move to tap me on the shoulder to see if I'd react.

"Come on," I said.

"Takako?" Giving one last look to my body, she jogged through the portal. The door closed silently behind her, before swirling into nothingness like a whirlpool.

I knew all this time that I was closing a portal, but I didn't realize I was closing a door.

And *another* thing!

I get to have an out-of-body experience, but the magical girls just come here as-is, putting themselves in danger?

Or—with the monsters out there with my unconscious body—am *I* the one who's in danger?

"Uh, Takako?" Hotaru's voice took me out of my thoughts. "Where are we?"

I rubbed my chin, looking at all the not-snow surrounding us, shining almost as brightly as the Red World had burned. "Well, there're two options—the *White* World or the *Iridescent* World." I looked back to her. "Take your pick."

Hotaru squinted and scrunched her freckled nose at me. "Why do *I* get to pick? You were the first one in here, so *you* decide." She crouched down and looked at the not-snow. "What *is* this stuff, anyway?" she muttered.

I crouched down next to her and picked up some of the mystery powder, rubbing my gloved hands together to filter out the finer grains. "It feels like...bones?" I opened my hands, and saw all the powder was gone, revealing a partial molar. "Specifically, teeth."

With that, Hotaru turned around and took a few paces away from me, then circled back when she realized there was no escaping from the unfortunate floor. "Takako. *Why* are we here? *Why* is everything *teeth?*" She shuddered, clearly creeped out from the whole situation.

I don't blame you.

I looked up at the Icicles. "I *guess* those are giant teeth, then? What are the pointy ones? Incisors?" I hummed to myself: *No, that doesn't seem right...though I guess it explains why it's not cold here.*

"Does it *matter?* It doesn't answer *why.*"

"Look," I sighed. "You want to leave, right?"

Hotaru nodded.

"Okay—so do I! The only way to get out is for you to fight the Icicles...or Incisors...whatever you wanna call them."

"No. Nope. No way."

"Come *on,* Hotaru. You're already *transformed...* We're already *here...* Might as well *try...*"

"Takako. My luck's been *horrible* lately." She circled around and made to sit down, but decided against it, instead shifting her weight from foot to foot, her arms crossed. "This is *stupid.*"

"And *I* said that your luck is going to *change.*" I took a deep breath. *If the universe *wants* me to be a magical girl so badly, I'll *act* like one—morals and all.* "Of *course* if you expect your luck to be bad, it'll be bad. Stop creating your downfall with a self-fulfilling prophecy."

"But I—"

I couldn't stop the motivational speech that spilled from my lips: *You're wallowing, hoping that someone will change your luck for you.*

What am I even *saying?* Is any of this even *true?*

"If you want your luck to change, you have to change it." I cocked my hip and put a victory sign to my eye. "That's the magical girl way!"

Hotaru's eyes widened, glistening with hope.

I brought my hands to my heart and then opened my arms in one grand gesture. "Now, are you ready to fight?"

Hotaru nodded, but before I could give her any further instruction, she pushed me to the side—or at least, tried to. Instead, she phased through my body and rolled into the powdery teeth. "Takako, dodge!"

"What?" I looked up to see an Icicle right above me, trembling.

I sidestepped before it crashed to the ground—right where I had been standing. Shockingly, the Icicle was about my height.

The other Icicles in the vicinity must have taken this as their cue and started sliding in our direction, shaking as they prepared to fall.

Very polite of them to wait for me to finish my inspirational speech.

Hotaru ran away as they crashed. "Get *out* of there, Takako!"

"Hotaru, use your powers!"

"Which would *be?*"

"Uh..." I thought back to her article in the magazine. "Grab a marshmallow from your belt?"

"A *marshmallow.* What's that gonna *do?* You want me to *baby-proof* these spikes so they don't poke anyone's eyes out?"

"Trust me!"

She rolled her eyes but still did as she was told and ripped a marshmallow off her belt—though it came off whole, not showing any sign of being torn from the garland. A new marshmallow spawned in its place.

"What should I do—"

Before she could finish this question, a skewer the length of her arm extended from her palm, piercing the soft cylinder. She gripped the handle and looked up at the marshmallow, perplexed.

"Okay, so now what—"

Once again, she was interrupted, this time as the marshmallow burst into flames.

"*Oh.*"

"You *know* what to do."

Hotaru looked up at the approaching Icicles and reached up, swatting at them with the flexible skewer as though she was reaching with a swatter for a bug on the ceiling that was just out of reach.

"Not those—*those.*" I pointed at the Icicles that had crashed. Somehow they had melted and reformed into stalagmites, and were now moving forward in her direction.

"Oh, *crap!*" Hotaru prodded them with the burning stick. One by one, they didn't melt—but collapsed in on themselves...sinking into the soft, broken teeth that made up the ground.

The whole skewer went up in flames, starting from the tip and making its way down to where Hotaru held it. Her hand was unaffected by the flames, but she was still startled and shook it out.

"So, what do I do about the monsters up there?"

"Take the baubles out of your ponytail and throw them." After picking up the pudding cups and opening one, I scouted ahead to find out where all of these Icicles were coming from. "Throw them at anything up there that seems out of the ordinary, too."

"Anything out of the ordinary. Besides the giant Icicles-maybe-teeth."

"Right."

Hotaru backflipped away from the falling Icicles. Then, she pulled the baubles from her hair and threw them at a random spot in the ceiling that looked like a crack—with condensation slowly dripping in the shape of a uvula.

The orange spheres exploded on contact, and when the smoke cleared, the crack was gone, leaving a black scorch mark in its place.

She turned to me. "Since they're not really ice, why would there be water dripping from the ceiling, right? Could be..." She cringed. "...drool?"

I crossed my arms and brought up a gloved hand to my chin in thought. "Yeah. That had to be one of the places where they're coming from. If you destroy all of them, no more Icicles can form."

"Good to know."

Hotaru ran back into the fray. The Icicles she had dodged on her way to destroy the spawner now acted as stalagmites, so she took another marshmallow off her belt and summoned the skewer. She fenced with her non-humanoid enemies, and after she won each bout, her opponent caved in on itself in defeat.

"How was that?" she asked, breathlessly.

Not bad, I said through a mouthful of pudding. "There were a couple of close calls, though. I didn't think you were going to make it past some of them."

Hotaru glared back at me. "It's my first time being a magical girl, *sheesh!* Give me a *break!*"

"I would, but there're more monsters."

I would, but there're more monsters—she mimicked. "That's how you sound."

I licked the spoon. "Doubt it."

"Yeah, well..." Hotaru adjusted her ponytail as the baubles reappeared in her hair. "At least I'm doing something about them," she grumbled.

"Anyway, as I was saying—there're more monsters," I repeated, electing to ignore her.

"And all I gotta do is find the rest of the leaks and blow them up? *Easy.*"

"You also have to defeat all the Icicles. If you miss any, you'll still have to fight them as you fight the giant one." The pudding cup fell from my hand, disappearing before it hit the ground.

"Yeah, and if it's anything like these, it'll be *easy.*"

"Really getting cocky, aren't you?"

"You haven't seen me race against Nana in P.E. yet—this is *nothing.*"

"Well, I wouldn't recommend getting too competitive here—if you don't defeat enough Icicles, I'll have you jump back down to the beginning to get them."

"*Back* down?"

"Yeah. There are a few more levels above us—it's like we're on the bottom shelf of a bookcase."

"How do you know all this?"

"When I was telling you to look for anything out of the ordinary, I saw that the ceiling doesn't go on forever in all directions. It just...stops." I pointed. "Over there."

It was blink-and-you-miss-it...but the flat, white ceiling ended, meeting sky of the same—or a very similar—color. Like comparing the white of paper to the white of snow.

Or teeth.

Hotaru walked over to the division and looked up. There were multiple platforms, perfectly aligned. It *would* be a long way down from the top...

"Wait..." She turned back to me. "You said the *giant* one..." She squinted. "You mean there's a single Icicle that's bigger than all the others? Like...an Alpha?"

I tilted my head. "Yes?"

"Soooooo... If it's bigger, then shouldn't it be heavier? Won't it just fall immediately? And then I can kill it in one shot? That's easy, right?"

"Once you cross the threshold to target that one specifically, it will summon all the Icicles that you haven't destroyed. And as you've seen, they fall at unpredictable rates." I lifted my chin, indignantly. "So yeah—it will *just fall*. But it won't be a one-hit kill, and you'll easily get outnumbered."

"*Great.*"

oo6

"So why can't I work with those other two magical girls?" Hotaru asked, catching her breath. She flopped down in the tooth-powder that the giant Icicle left behind upon its defeat, too tired to care anymore that it wasn't actually snow.

The plants and water girls, she clarified—as if she needed to.

I pondered this for a moment. "They're using their paid vacation days."

Hotaru bolted upright. "Wait, that's a *thing?*"

I blinked down at her. "*No.*"

She slumped back into the not-ice, and some particles flew up on impact. She blew out a puff of air to avoid having the cloud disperse and come back down on her face.

"Jeez, why d'you gotta *be* like that, Takako?"

"There's just not enough power to go around," I replied, ignoring her last question in favor of the first.

"Then why don't you—y'know—*not* transform? And transform me and someone else—like Nana, 'cause you're not really doing much to help me."

"*I* have to transform in order to transform someone else. Like your power is *fire,* my power is...*creation.*"

"Sure, I *guess* that makes sense..."

"I've *also* been gathering up the pudding and flan you *carelessly* left behind."

"Right..."

"Not to mention..." I sat down in the tooth-powder next to her, hugging my legs and resting my chin on my knees. "I helped you with the burnout from your bugaboo."

"Ah, yeah." Hotaru rolled over to face away from me. "Yeah, thanks for that..." Her words sounded awkward.

If her ears weren't covered by her costume, would they be turning red from embarrassment?

"By the way, I meant what I said." What was it that I even said? The start of this whole battle felt like it was so long ago...but I know that little to no time passed since we entered the portal. My speech was so "spur-of-the-moment" that I didn't put much thought into it.

"Yeah, my luck's gonna change, 'cause I'm gonna change it." Hotaru sighed, then turned to look at me. "Honestly, when you first said that, I didn't think about it that hard."

Gee. Thanks.

It's the magical girl way—she imitated me. "It just... It seemed *fake*—too good to be true, y'know? But at the same time, you had the *confidence* behind it. You're a *real* magical girl. *I'm* a real magical girl! And then, I actually fought *monsters*—and I won!"

I had *confidence* when I said that?

Well, fake it until you—

"Canines!" I exclaimed.

Hotaru jolted upright from her self-reflection. "*Huh?*"

"The pointy teeth aren't incisors. They're *canines*." I thumped my forehead with the heel of my hand, feeling stupid for not remembering.

"That doesn't really matter anymore, does it? I mean, they're gone. I'm not gonna have to fight them again any time soon, right?"

"Hm." My smile faded into a straight line. "Yeah, I guess you're right."

And now not only do I feel stupid for *not* remembering it earlier...but also for bringing it up *now*.

Way to go, Takako.

Way.

To.

Go.

"So…" Hotaru stretched as she stood and tilted her head at the door—same size that the others had been, but textured with a snowflake's fractals. "Is that the exit?"

"Yeah. Ready to go?"

"Yeah." She blinked—then widened her stance, mussing up her hair. "Crap! *Nana!*" Hotaru combed one hand's fingers through her bangs. "Oh, crap! I totally forgot! Is she gonna be okay?"

"She's fine—don't worry."

"How can you be *sure* though?" Hotaru squeezed my arms. "She was *frozen solid!*" Her eyes widened. "Someone could've come into the classroom and toppled her, and shattered her, and—isn't that a thing that can happen?"

"Hotaru!" I pried her fingers away. "She's *fine*. I mean…" Should I tell her? Sure, why not? "*You* were fine when a *Water Droplet* swallowed *you* whole."

"What."

"So you really *don't* remember… I had a feeling. On my first day here, you got caught in the rain after school—that's probably what you remember. But you were *really* absorbed by a *monster*."

"*W-What?*" Hotaru clutched her head. "No…" She screwed her eyes shut. "It definitely *was* raining…but then why do I…"

I patted her hunched shoulder. She looked up at me.

"Takako…"

"Come on, let's go." Was this the right thing to do?

"Why do I remember two things happening at the same time?"

Now that she's a magical girl, will she remember the monster attacks going forward?

Will she remember the Fire Flares from the library, too?

What could have gone on in there while Youko was in battle?

"It's a worse headache than the time I was dehydrated on Sports Day…" Hotaru winced. "I'm seeing double…"

I held my arm around the small of her back and helped her stumble to the door. "It's okay…"

Is it, though?

Hotaru stepped over the threshold, and suddenly I was back in my body, looking up at her from the classroom floor. Nana was no longer affixed to the ground in ice—instead, she was sitting at her desk, dozing off.

Hotaru let out a quiet sigh. "Nana, you're—"

I hushed at her as I stood up. "You can't tell her *anything* that just happened—not about the monster attack, not being a magical girl. *Nothing.*"

"I...I can't keep all that a secret." She gestured at her friend. "Nana has the right to know about how she was frozen!"

"And what would knowing accomplish?" I asked. "When I told you about the Water Droplets, you were in *pain.* Do you want *her* to feel that?"

Hotaru sucked in her cheeks in thought. "I *guess* you're right...but I *really* don't like keeping stuff from her."

Nana stretched at her desk. "Wow, it's *chilly.*" She turned to the window, which was still wide open. In her mini sweep of the room, she glanced over us. "Hotaru! Takako? What...happened?"

Before I could come up with an excuse, Hotaru asked: *What do you remember?*

Nana squeezed her eyes shut. "I was at the window, and..." She tilted her head. "I *guess* someone was upstairs, clapping erasers." She let out a small huff at Hotaru. "And *you* tricked me into thinking it was snowing, so I got covered in chalk dust. Ha *ha.* Not funny, didn't laugh."

"Well, we're even now—for not getting caught in the rain with me last month, you *coward.*"

"Not *my* fault you're slower than me!"

"But it *is* your fault that you weren't polite—and who're you calling slow? *You're* so slow, your hair's turtle-colored!"

"Hey, I got your gym clothes for you to change into! And *excuse* me? *Your* hair's so red, it's telling you to *stop!*"

"It's the *principle!* And *I* beat you in our last dash, or did you already forget?"

I sighed and walked over to the window to close it...but not before noticing white dust on the outside of the glass.

Teeth being mistaken for Icicles, and in turn the universe's excuse is chalk dust.

I guess teeth and chalk have calcium in common, but why couldn't *Magical Girl Monthly* just *call* them Teeth from the start?

Maybe it was to avoid scaring me away from the battle?

Magical girl logic.

I slung my bag over my shoulder and walked out of the classroom, electing for Hotaru and Nana to work things out on their own...

Hopefully not revealing their secret identities to each other in the process.

OO7

"What's…" Suzu woke up and didn't recognize the ceiling as her own. "Where is this?" she asked, panic setting in.

She turned her head and sank further into the pillow.

The dimly lit room seemed to have more shadows than light. There couldn't possibly be anyone in the dark, waiting there to answer her questions when she woke up…right?

She was wrong.

Deadly Omen Finders' Headquarters, Gorgeous replied—leaning against the wall just out of Suzu's line of sight.

The young girl recoiled and tried to sit up…but found that she was restrained to the bed. "*Mizuki!*"

"Don't call me that!" she spat. "You all betrayed me!"

"No…"

"Yes! Do you even realize how *difficult* it was to bring you here?" Her heels clicked as she walked to the bedside. "I had to let the Deadly Omen you fought escape to ensure that your so-called *friends* and *pets* wouldn't follow us."

"You *kidnapped* me!"

"Did I *really?*" Gorgeous gripped Suzu's chin and reached over to the side table for a small dish of broth. "*Did* I, now? *I* see it more like *this*—we're taking preventative measures against another Omen's creation. So is that how you should be *thanking* your savior?"

"S-Savior?"

The one who is changing your fate? Gorgeous continued. She held the dish to Suzu's lips, forcing the girl to swallow.

Suzu spluttered and thrashed about but couldn't get the dish to budge.

"You became a *Goddess* to *extend* your life?" Gorgeous asked. "I have to laugh."

Okay, there's *definitely* more broth in the dish than it can possibly hold...

But that's *anime* logic for you.

"The Elves aren't telling the *truth*. Your life may be extended...but there is a *cost*."

Finally, the supply of broth dwindled, and Gorgeous placed the dish on the table with a light *clink*.

"*I* was in your position, Suzu," she whispered, voice cracking.

Suzu opened her mouth to question this but could only *gurgle*.

"The Deadly Omen Finders..." Gorgeous sat down on the edge of the bed and lightly touched the back of Suzu's hand. "They *saved* me. And *I'm* going to save *you*."

So...the antagonists aren't really villains?

Huh. What a twist.

I brought my legs up, curling them tightly under my blanket as I ate another spoonful of pudding.

"*Why* are you doing this?" Suzu was finally able to cry out, softly.

"Because I love my little sister."

I winced as the spoon clicked against my teeth.

"Are you..."

"No, *you're* not my sister," Gorgeous replied, rolling her eyes. "The Elves promise many things. Life. Love. Fame. Wealth. Power. Then, they keep making promises. Promises pile up, Suzu. They promised they would help my sister—on top of all the other promises they made, of course—but..."

As if on cue, a spotlight turned on at the other side of the room, revealing a young girl—younger than Suzu—in a tank filled with a viscous liquid. Her wavy brown hair—as long as she was tall—billowed around her, and her white summer dress rippled from the occasional air bubble entering the base of the tank.

"She's..."

"*Elegant*—my sister, Aimi." Gorgeous pulled her gaze away from her sister to look at Suzu. "And *also* what you'll become if you keep listening to the Elves."

I gulped, dropping my spoon into a half-empty pudding cup.
Am I leading my classmates to a fate similar to...
To whatever *this* is?
No, this is fiction.

Episode Four
Manami Suits

OOI

Thursday, May thirteenth. For some reason, my desk had become *the* go-to meeting spot for magical girl discussions during lunch, regardless of if I was eating there or on the roof.

Tsubasa had turned her chair around to face my desk. Miku had pulled a chair from another desk, but instead of sitting, she stood while resting a leg on it, half-kneeling. Masuyo stood next to her. Nana leaned against the neighboring desk, while Hotaru was slumped over in a borrowed chair, fading in and out of a nap. I leaned back in my chair.

"So anyway, I *was* close with my guess...my proposed order was just off by one!" Miku said, munching on a triangle-shaped sandwich. "She had fire powers. The next magical girl is *definitely* gonna have control over air!"

Maybe—Tsubasa said, shrugging. "Who's to say? There are other possible powers."

"Yeah, *no*. Earth—I'm counting the plants girl as earth, because it's nature—water, fire...and then air." Miku took a final swig from her can of juice. "I mean, these are traditional elements to have control over in fiction. It's not like there'll be a magical girl with power over—let's see—sulfur, or any other element from the periodic table!"

"*I* believe it will be a team of *five*." Masuyo wrote in their notepad.

"There *must* be a leader who has the power of *love!*"

Miku spluttered. "*Love?* No. Honestly, I never got how someone's power could be an abstract concept like that." She tightened her grip in an attempt to crush her can. "Call me when there's a magical girl who can rip out her *heart* and *throw* it at someone. Ha—*that's* the closest you'd get to a magical girl's 'power of love' in real life."

"Wow, what a *romantic,*" Tsubasa chimed in.

"Well—excuse *me*—but how else could the 'power of love' appear as something physical?!" Miku exclaimed, face contorting in frustration.

Before Tsubasa could answer, Masuyo placed their pad down on Tsubasa's desk and hugged Miku from the side, nuzzling her neck.

The dented can fell from Miku's grasp and clattered to the ground.

Nana snorted, but pretended to cough to cover it up.

"Was that physical enough for you?" Masuyo chirped as they pulled away from the blue-haired girl.

Before the sandwich could also fall, Tsubasa snatched it and placed it in Miku's gaping mouth like a giant makeshift pacifier. I could practically see the smoke exiting from Miku's head as she short-circuited.

Nana failed to hide her snorts behind her hand.

"So, what was the fire magical girl like?" I asked, scraping pudding off the side of the cup with my spoon. "I didn't see the video."

Masuyo reached for a small bag on an adjacent desk, and opened it to reveal a camcorder.

I raised an eyebrow.

"I saved the file to my memory card," they explained. "Youko would confiscate my phone, but not this...since it is *technically* club property!"

I sneaked a peek over at Youko—she was sitting at her desk, eating lunch and not paying us any heed.

Masuyo navigated to a video before handing me the camera.

Looking down at the small screen, I saw Hotaru—fighting Icicles right outside the school gates.

I glanced at her over Masuyo's shoulder.

The redhead blinked slowly...starting with one glazed eye and then the other.

"I really think we should give the magical girls names," Tsubasa suggested. "It sounds awkward just to tack on their power to 'magical girl'—they need hero names!"

"Hero names? What did you have in mind?" Miku asked, finally pulled out of her hug-induced trance.

"Well, let's start with the first one." Tsubasa crossed her arms. "Since she had power over plants—"

"*Earth,*" Miku corrected.

"Until she shows up again and hurls a *rock* at a villain, I'm calling it—her power is over *plants.*"

"*So,* what's *your* name for her, then?" Miku asked, a vice grip on her sandwich triangle.

"Veggie Girl!"

I looked over to Nana. Her face was blank until she caught my gaze, and without blinking she muttered: *I laid this bamboo against the bamboo fence because I wanted to lay bamboo against it.*

"Yeah..." Tsubasa's shoulders hunched, and she tilted her head to the side, wilting. "I know—it *sucks.*"

"No!" Nana exclaimed as she pushed off the desk and tried to reassure her. "It's just...why don't we wait for *her* to reveal her name? Next time she appears, she'll probably introduce herself since she was caught on camera...right?"

She's gaining popularity, she added. "Right?"

I blinked. Why are you asking *me?* "Popularity?"

"Yeah!" Tsubasa beamed, nodding in agreement. "All of the magical girl videos have been getting popular online—to the point they're being broadcast on TV!"

"Fujioka High School's Seventh Mystery is gaining traction throughout the city," Masuyo added. "As a paranormal researcher, I must say it is very exciting!"

"Ooh!" Tsubasa stood and slammed her hands on my desk. "That'd be a cool team name! *Seventh Mystery!*"

"Wait, are they even a team?" Miku muttered, now finished with her sandwich and removing crumbs from under her nails. "I know *I've* been the one speculating that they're a team of four or five—but they've never even been seen together in the same place. Shouldn't we wait until they've actually *fought together* against a common enemy before we jump to the conclusion that they're a team?"

Tsubasa and Masuyo looked at her, blankly.

"Fine! *Seventh Mystery* it is!" Miku crossed her arms. "It's gonna *annoy* me since there aren't seven magical girls...but sure! *Whatever!*"

Tsubasa spun around, and cheered in an announcer voice, "Plants Mystery! Water Mystery! Fire Mystery!" She crouched down, bending one arm near her head and sticking the other out to the side. In this pose, she exclaimed, "Together, they make up the Seventh Mystery of Fujioka High School! What foe will they defeat next? Tune in next week to find out!"

I looked over at Hotaru, who had fallen into a deep sleep at some point during this conversation.

Oh, it's going to be *much* sooner than next week...

OO2

Kenji crawled through the Darkness on his hands and knees to one of many piles of twisted toys and broken playthings. He muttered to himself occasionally as he riffled through his stuff, throwing things behind him...only for them to not crash, instead resetting to another position in his hoard.

"Oh, your snow cone machine broke?" Miyako asked from the shadows, picking at her teeth. She was a silhouette, as though the shadows were a thin coating on her skin, hair, and clothes.

Even with his sight perfectly adjusted to the Darkness, Kenji couldn't make out her face.

But it was okay—he was used to it.

Besides, even with no shadows covering it, half of Miyako's face was obscured by her long bangs.

"Shit," she continued. "I was *really* hopin' for a snow cone. Somethin' *sweet* that's served *cold!*" Miyako cackled—a grating sound. "Just *desserts!*"

Kenji glared into the Darkness—directly at her.

"Fine! *Fine!* Black cherry would've been good, too!"

"It's *broken* and can't be *fixed!*" he shouted, still glaring. He picked up a wooden ball on a string—once part of a *kendama,* but now frayed at the end from sharpened teeth—and threw it at her.

"Yeah, yeah. I *know.*" Miyako ducked out of the way just in time. "No matter *what* I give to my *Little Brother Dearest,* it won't last till the end of the day." She took a few steps closer. "So—whatcha wanna do now?"

"I *want* to *go.*"

Miyako spluttered. "*Whaaaat?*" She bent over, hands on her knees, as though his suggestion winded her. "Nah, you're not goin' *anywhere.* Mama and *Daddy Dearest* would *kill* me." She leaned back and crossed her arms. "Hm... How *intriguing...*"

"I *want* to *leave!*" Kenji stamped his foot. "I'm *bored!*"

"You've got toys, though!" Miyako spread out her arms, gesturing at the pile her brother currently sat in. "Look at all of 'em. There's gotta be *somethin'* that ya haven't played with in a while!"

"They're not *special!*" Kenji shouted.

Miyako snorted. "You're such a *child.* Your toys are special only when *you* make them special."

"Shut *up!* I *hate* you!"

Kenji found himself lifted by the collar over his sister's head.

"Put me down!" the boy screamed, legs flailing in the air as he tried to kick her. "Put me *down, Miyako!"

"You want a new toy that badly, Baby Bro? *And* ya wanna leave? You don't realize how much it is you're really askin' for."

With that, Miyako dropped him back in the pile and turned on her heel, long hair swishing behind her.

Kenji—sensing that he was now alone in the Darkness—shrieked, smashing his hands on his throne of junk.

Beneath his right hand was a box of cards.

Smooth.

The cardboard wasn't frayed—it was brand new, the seal unbroken.

Mint condition.

Not for long.

Kenji picked it up as he stood and held it over his head, then slammed the box into the ground.

He picked it up and did it a second time.

And a third.

"You *never* let me do *anything* I want!" he shouted. "None of you do!"

The corners of the box wrinkled with each collision against the ground.

"I want a toy! I wanna go somewhere! *Anywhere* is better than *here!*"

He kicked the box to the side so hard that it split open. The cards scattered all over the ground.

"I hate it here! I *hate* it!"

Kenji collapsed on the ground, face heating up with every sob.

One by one, the cards stood on end—paper thin obelisks shining in the Darkness.

OO3

Aki and Hikari stood up after finishing their lunch—to go do whatever it was popular girls did on break—when they crossed paths with Chou and Manami in the doorway.

"Hey—don't forget that it's *your* turn for cleaning duty after school, Fujioka," Chou growled.

Aki gasped, feigning ignorance. "Whaaaat? *Moi?*" She leaned down, getting in the cat girl's face. "No way—you *must* be mistaken."

"But I looked at the schedule! That's what it said!" Chou exclaimed, stomping her foot. "You *always* do this, *nya!*" She held up a clipboard that contained what I could only assume was the cleaning schedule.

"Fujioka Aki contributes *far* more to the school than you could ever dream of accomplishing, *Okuma,*" Hikari explained, snatching the clipboard from her.

Chou hissed, hair bristling up like a cat's.

Manami patted her friend on the shoulder. "I think what Chou's trying to say is, like...we don't really *see* Aki's contributions that much, y'know?"

"We've been *over* this, Manami!" Aki replied, flipping her hair. "My family *owns* the school. I'm able to influence major decisions!"

Hikari nodded, before showing off her uniform. "Behold—the

uniform of Fujioka High School."

Aki twirled around on her toes. "Designed by yours truly, at the age of eight."

"*I* was there to witness it," Hikari added. "A blue blazer and skirt to represent Fujioka's eyes. A gold sweater vest and a bow to represent her hair. A white shirt and brown loafers because, well, that's *standard*."

"Y'know how in shows and movies," Manami started slowly, finding her words, "you'll see girls that decide what high school to go to based on how cute the uniform is?"

"Yes!" Aki exclaimed, hand on her hip.

"I didn't choose to go here based on the uniform."

Hikari gasped.

"It's butt ugly!" Chou provided.

Aki's nostrils flared. "Well, I already *knew* that *you* have no taste!"

"I have taste! 'Nami says so!"

"Is that so?" Aki turned to the pink-haired gal, stepping so close to look down on her that I thought toes would be crushed. "In that case, it's *already* obvious to me that *you* don't have taste, either—seeing as you decided to cut ties with us last year because of this *chuuni*."

"I only left because *you* don't know when to *stop!*" Manami shouted, bracelets jangling. She took a step back so she wouldn't have to look up at an uncomfortable angle. "*God,* Aki. Hikari's like, *all* of your impulse control! You never think for yourself—you gave *her* all of your brain cells for safe keeping!"

Aki turned into a tomato as she sputtered.

I mean, from what I've seen it's true.

But Manami didn't have to *say* it.

"Now, now. We're all *mature* here," Hikari chimed in, before looking at Chou. "Well, *almost*." She glared at Manami and tilted her head, pigtails swaying. "There's no *need* for playground insults. The first to use them is clearly the loser, so it's safe to say this discussion is over. Wouldn't you agree, Takakuwa?"

Manami crossed her arms and shifted her weight to the side. "Maybe so, but like—you and Aki aren't exactly *disproving* my point right now."

Aki finally supplied her signature laugh. "*Everyone* knows brain cells can't be *given* away! You have to *buy* or *exchange* them like any other commodity!"

Hikari stared at her friend, dumbfounded. "That's—"

"Hikari's the personal assistant of my school life," Aki continued with her comeback. "She helps me organize my schedule as well as my thoughts, and in return I provide her with my family's connections."

"E-Exactly! Fujioka is too *busy* to worry about the little things in life, such as yourself and—to get back on topic—cleaning duty." Hikari made a few quick marks on the page before shoving it against Manami's chest. "Fujioka has a prior commitment for this afternoon, so *Okuma* will be taking her place."

Chou's mouth gaped open, tears welling in her eyes as she tried to argue...though all that came out was a stuttered: *B-B-But...*

"Thank you, Hikari," Aki said, heading out the door.

"It's my pleasure."

"But that's not *fair,*" Chou sniffed, wiping her tears with her sleeve. "I was gonna..."

"Just think of this as preparation for the *real* world." Hikari turned and gave Chou a smug smile. "When you have a job, there will be times when you won't get what you want. You'll have to make sacrifices."

OO4

No matter what I do, my copy of *Magical Girl Monthly* disappears at some point between the walk from school to my apartment.

This is a fact—one that I've been testing for these past three weeks.

Is the magazine tied to the school somehow?

A fail-safe so that I don't lose it?

At what point does it disappear from my bag?

The monster page updated for today—but with the school day having ended, I decided to run a test today.

As usual, I put the magazine in my bag as I got up from my desk.

Instead of shutting the bag and hoping for the best, I kept the zipper open *just* a bit.

Nonchalantly.

I changed into my loafers and wedged my hand into the opening of the bag up to my wrist, making sure I could feel the magazine's pages between my fingers.

And then, I ran into a problem.

With the bag on my shoulder and my hand jammed inside, I was suddenly giving my best impersonation of someone spliced vertically with a *T-Rex*.

Non-nonchalantly.

I sighed.

As I walked out of the school gates, I noticed Masuyo causing a commotion—waving their arm in the air, papers fluttering in their grasp.

"The Seventh Mystery! The Seventh Mystery!" they shouted. "We've *finally* found Fujioka High School's *Seventh Mystery!*"

"What are you doing?" I wondered aloud.

Masuyo turned to me, arm outstretched, pamphlet in hand. "Ah! Takako! Would you like to help me pass these out? *Everyone* needs to know about our school's Seventh Mystery!"

I turned to hide the hand in my bag. "They can watch the videos on the news and that site they were originally posted on, can't they?"

"Right you are! People *can* watch the videos, but they won't *know* they're *our* Seventh Mystery! We have to get the word out about their names, before companies try to sell merchandise with names like...oh, I don't know...*Veggie Girl.*"

And so, the truth comes out: Masuyo wasn't a fan of the name Tsubasa came up with, either.

"But what if the magical girls reveal their names later?" I asked. "Won't it be confusing for everyone?"

"That won't be an issue. I'm not really getting *anywhere* with these." They waved a handful of pamphlets at me.

Held in their other arm was a *very* thick stack.

How'd they print them all out so quickly?

Did they have a template ready, and only had to add the magical girl names after today's conversation?

"So far, only students from our school have taken them. A couple of teachers, too. So, if the magical girls *do* have introductions and a team name later on—it will be an easy fix."

I nodded and relented, reaching for the top pamphlet with my free hand.

They beamed at me before turning their attention to a salaryman.

Really hope that these names won't spread *too* far by word of mouth...

What if actual names get revealed later on in *Magical Girl Monthly?*

oo5

Opposite the school, the street was populated by shops—apparel, confectioneries, and other stores. In my time at Fujioka High School, there were a few things I learned about the town: Fujioka was purchased and renamed by Aki's parents. They offered a lot of jobs, free enrollment at the high school, reasonably priced housing…

How could a family so generous raise someone like Aki?

Maybe the Fujioka Kindness skips a generation—Nana had suggested when I posed the question.

"It's harder to be kind than it is to be mean," Masuyo had added. "Who knows what they're truly capable of when they drop the façade?"

"There's no façade," Miku replied. "It's obvious that they were so kind to Aki—she became spoiled. Like overdoing a pancake!"

"At this point, are they even aware of how she acts?" Tsubasa had asked. "You'd think people as kind as them would step in if they caught wind of her behavior. Guess they're just blind to it."

I walked down the street about a block when I refocused and realized I was still holding onto *Magical Girl Monthly*.

How far away from the school can I walk until it disappears from my grasp?

Does it disappear when I enter my apartment?

Is it so I can't study it outside of school?

But why would that be the case, if its goal is to help me defeat the monsters? Wouldn't it *want* me to be ready for anything?

The smell of freshly ground coffee wafted by my nose, and I stopped in my tracks.

There's no real need for me to get back home *immediately*...right?

It's Thursday and I have homework, but I can stop for a hot cup of coffee...yeah?

It was then that I heard the scream and knew the Tutorial Goddesses had abandoned me.

Something brushed against my calves, grumbling and muttering to itself. I looked down and saw a spade—not the gardening tool, but the playing card symbol.

Completely flat—if not for the slight angle and its shadow, I would've missed it.

It looked up at me with big eyes—located at the curved part of its body—before scampering to the middle of the road to meet its friends—more spades, in addition to clubs. How can something scamper without limbs?

Some of the monsters were piled on top of each other—as though a giant had started a game of 52-card pickup.

"Okay..." I murmured to myself.

Besides the obvious traffic hazard, this almost seems like a non-issue.

A cleanup crew could come in and just...

Sweep these guys away, right?

I turned around and saw Manami, school bag in one hand and strawberry bubble tea in the other—backing away not from the monsters, but from the clothing store she just stepped out of.

Clothing racks and the bodies of customers—no, those are just mannequins—barricaded the doors.

"Manami! Over here!"

She blinked her dark pink eyes, like she was surprised to see me. "T-Takako?"

I walked over to her with caution, intending to pull her away from the road, but she hoisted her bag onto her shoulder and grabbed my wrist before I could act.

146

"Oh my *God,* am I glad to *see* you!" Manami exclaimed. "I usually know what to expect when they have sales, but *that...* I've never seen *anything* like that!"

"Yeah, that's nice," I said, trying to take a step back.

"*Nice?*" Her eyes widened. "Takako! I'm pretty sure someone threw, like...a *chair!* At a *person!*"

"Okay, well, can we continue this somewhere else? There's something going on here..."

Manami blinked, then turned slightly...finally noticing the carnage on the road.

The monsters simultaneously took a step forward, letting out a loud *shhk*—like a deck being shuffled.

"Move!" I grabbed her by the wrist and ran.

"W-Where are we *going?*"

I shrugged the best I could while running, making the sound associated with it. "Somewhere without those things, I guess!"

"You *guess?*"

"*I guess!*"

A block away, we ducked into an alley and stopped to catch our breath.

"What *are* those things, Takako? They look like...like, I dunno...upside-down hearts? Heads of broccoli?"

"Spades and clubs—they're Suits."

"Yeah, I *know,* but can you, like, even *blame* me for forgetting the words when we were just, like...running for our *lives?*"

"Sorry..."

Manami sighed and leaned against the wall, bag falling to her elbow.

This reminded me to look in *my* bag to make sure the magazine was still there—in the rush, I'd let go of it, and we were now two blocks from the school.

After confirming that the magazine hadn't vanished, I looked up and saw that Manami was taking out her phone.

"Uh, what are you doing?"

"One of the magical girls is probably gonna show up, right?" She held up her phone, camera app open. "*So,* I'm gonna record 'em and upload the vid myself!" She brought the straw to her lips and muttered:

Monetization, here I come.

"But what if a magical girl *doesn't* show up?"

"There's like...*three* of 'em. There's a pretty *good* chance *one* of them'll show." Manami took a sip from her tea. "Maybe I'll even get some footage of a *new* girl! Or even the whole team! Seventh Mystery—seen together for the first time ever!" She giggled. "Won't Masuyo be *jealous?*"

I stared at her, raising an eyebrow.

After a few long slurps, the pink-haired girl placed her phone on her bag and started absently poking at the pearls in her tea with the straw. "They're...not comin', are they?"

"No."

"*Great.*" Manami became bored with the pearls and set the cup down on the sidewalk.

"But *you* could become a magical girl."

"*Excuse* me?"

"You heard me."

"Uhh, I don't know *what* I heard. Mind saying it again?"

"I could turn you into a magical—"

"*Yes.*"

"You really took no time to think it over, huh? What happened to worrying about 'exams and college'?"

"Honestly? Who *cares* about that stuff? I'm gonna be a *magical girl!*" Manami hitched her bag onto her shoulder and held out her hand, expectantly. "So, do I get a trinket or somethin'? Like, a pen? Or maybe, like, a ring? I mean, I've got *waaayyy* too many bracelets, so that might get a little confusing...but it'd also be a perfect cover for my alter ego!"

She closed her eyes and beamed at me.

I took *Magical Girl Monthly* out of my bag, tore a strip from the correct page, and placed it in her upturned palm.

Her grabby fingers closed around it, and she opened her eyes.

"What's this?" she asked, flatly.

"It's your catalyst to transform."

"*Hah?!*" Manami brought the paper close to her eyes.

It was pink, with faint white outlines of cartoon hearts scattered about.

Upon further inspection, one could say the hearts' placement wasn't random, and possibly meant to evoke the outline of a realistic heart's ventricles...though I could be reading too much into it.

"Ya mean...after wanting to be a magical girl—for like, my *entire life*—all I get's a *piece of paper?*"

"Trinket machine's broken."

Manami gasped. "There's a *machine?*"

I did an internal facepalm. "*No.*"

I went through my usual spiel as I transformed, and then watched as the paper flew up from her hand and expanded, becoming a translucent infinity scarf around her shoulders. A pink light emanated from it.

When the light subsided, she stood before me in a short, pale pink, strapless dress, with a large, white ribbon tied around her waist, a small heart printed on her stomach. She wore dark pink, fingerless gloves that ended right below her shoulders. Her socks were white thigh highs, each with their own small heart on the front near the hem. Her dark pink ankle boots had chunky but fashionable heels. To top it all off, she had heart-shaped discs in her hair buns—and only now have I realized her hair buns have been styled to look like hearts this entire time!

"Welcome," I said, "to the Seventh Mystery of Fujioka High School." I did my best to give a grand gesture as I knelt, but it probably came off as sarcastic.

Especially since I'm still not a fan of the name supplied by my classmates.

Masuyo and Tsubasa will probably be ecstatic if it's revealed—but it'll probably implicate everyone involved in that conversation as possible magical girls.

Wow, I didn't think this—

Manami tapped my shoulder. "So...where'd my bag go? And my drink?"

I considered this for a moment, before answering: *I don't know.*

"Well, what about that paper? When I transform back, am I gonna be holding, like, a piece of paper?"

It was then that I realized I hadn't been paying attention after the battles and had no idea what happened to the papers.

Where *did* they go?

Once through the door—post-battle—did it reappear in a pocket? In a bag?

"Like, what happens if my mom says she's gonna clean my room, and she throws it away? It's just a scrap of *paper,* so she'd *def* toss it! Would you tear another piece for me? Or would I be outta luck and not be able to transform? Or, I dunno," Manami said, crouching to get on my level, "will I *die?*"

"You are *not* going to die." I patted her shoulder in an attempt to comfort her. "*Trust* me."

Manami bit her lip, then released it and let out a breath to calm down. "I...I know it's kinda childish, but sometimes Chou'll make me do it..." She held up her fist, then extended her pinky. "Will you *promise* me that I won't die?"

I looked down at her finger, and realized I had to make a split-second decision:

She doesn't know what the battles are like—and I don't know what the battles will be like in the future. *Can* someone die? There have been a few close calls, but...

I linked my pinky with Manami's. "I promise."

Crash!

Our little moment was interrupted by shattered glass, followed by the sounds of a roaring mob.

"Uh...Takako? What's that?"

The mob's out-of-sync footfalls came closer to our alley, and Manami clutched my shoulder—I just about thought she was going to hide behind me, curled up on the ground.

"The effect of the Suits. It's weird..." I mused. "The previous monsters all had effects on the physical world, but these seem to be affecting people's *minds?*"

"So you're telling me that I gotta fight *people?* I can't hurt them, Takako! Even *if* one of 'em is guilty of throwing a chair at someone!"

"You're not going to fight *them,* don't worry." I placed my hand over my heart and tipped my head forward, focusing on opening the portal.

Manami looked at it for a moment, then stood and walked a circle around it.

I expected to lose sight of her from my place in the other world, but

150

this was not the case—my view shifted to follow her, as if we were in some big musical montage of her trying on clothes, and I was following her around with a fancy mirror on wheels.

"Come *on*." I gestured. "Did you already forget that we have company?" Over her shoulder, I could see the crowd approaching.

With a high-pitched squeak, Manami jumped through the portal, crashing into me. We tumbled to the ground.

"Oof! Sorry, Takako!" She stood up and offered me her hand—in the completely wrong direction.

I refused it and stood up by myself.

I furrowed my brow. Since when am I corporeal here?

Thinking back, I guess I *did* interact with the tooth-powder last time...and in the end, didn't I pat Hotaru on the back?

Am I getting more powerful, able to interact with these worlds?

"Where are we?" Manami nibbled her thumbnail. "It's so dark...like, you wouldn't happen to know where the light switch is, huh?"

"It's the Black World." I took a few steps forward.

It wasn't that we were in the dark—the floor, walls, and ceiling appeared to be painted pitch black.

Something scuttled in the distance, around a corner.

Is this a maze?

"Yeah, I can *see* that. Well—no, I *can't*—but like, you probably knew that already."

Okay, maybe *I'm* not in total darkness—but my magical girl companion definitely is. "I'm over here, Manami."

She turned in the general direction of my voice. "How am I supposed to fight if I can't *see* anything? Oh God, Takako..." She sniffled and wiped her nose with the back of her gloved hand. (Gross.) "I don't wanna *die*..."

"I already promised you that you won't die. Hold on..." I walked behind her and placed my hand on her shoulder.

"*Eeeep!*" Manami swatted my hand away. "Monster!"

"It's just me." I gave her shoulder a firm pat. "Face that way and blow a kiss."

"*Huh?*"

"*Trust* me."

Manami pressed two fingers to her lips and unfurled her arm. A pink cartoon heart squeezed its way out from between her lips like it was made of bubblegum and floated along the length of her arm—growing in size as it drifted away and phased through the wall.

The scuttling on the other side stopped, replaced by an ear-piecing *ee-ee-ee!*

"Takako..." Manami slowly turned to face me. "What was *that...?*"

"A Suit." I released Manami's shoulder, but at the sound of more scuttling in our direction, she immediately leaned back in my direction.

Please don't let go, she murmured.

"I'm right by your side." I spun her back around, placing one hand on her left shoulder and the other on her right forearm. She clasped her hands together, and from their shared grip emerged a white, papery staff, telescoping outward in two directions.

"Wow..." Manami looked upwards, finally seeing something in this dark world—a flat, pink heart on the end of the staff.

The staff was visible through the glassy heart, stopping midway through it. Air bubbles surrounded the staff in the glass.

"So...do I eat it?"

"No, you hit monsters with it."

Manami took a step away and turned to face me, her eyes focused. "Why couldn't I see anything in here before getting this?"

"It's obvious, isn't it?" Come on, Takako—think of a stereotypical magical girl speech! "You were blinded by hatred."

"Wait, but like...why would *I* be blinded by *hatred?* And how? Isn't my power, like, the power of love?"

"Yes." I didn't attempt to elaborate, and I must've made an expression that indicated I didn't intend to, as Manami pursed her lips and turned back when she heard more distant shuffling sounds.

A swarm of Suits shuffled in from around the corner. Before I could give her any further instruction, Manami took a running start and brought the lollipop scepter down on the Suits—doing a split midair.

Once she landed, she hit a few more Suits to the side like croquet balls, though her form—complete with follow-through—was more like a golfer's.

I crossed my arms. "Huh."

"What?"

"You're just really *good* at this, that's all."

"I mean...I *told* you I wanted to be a magical girl!"

"That you did, Manami. That you did."

Manami blew a kiss to more Suits rounding the corner, and they dropped like flies.

I scouted ahead and caught a glimpse of a thin box folding shut. It was like someone had built a brick wall, but had forgotten a brick near the bottom and someone had left the box for a deck of cards there in its place, sticking out.

Of course, a deck with only two suits would make for a boring—and definitely rigged—game.

"Whatcha lookin' at?" Manami leaned over my shoulder.

"Gah!" Regaining my composure, I turned and hushed her.

Once more, the box opened. Another Suit slid out, landing on its short tail.

Shuuschk!

I blinked, and in that millisecond it slid towards us—too close.

"Monster!" Manami exclaimed and slammed the Suit into the floor with her lollipop scepter.

"Did you see where it came from?" I asked. The box's flaps fluttered. "Destroy that, and it won't be able to create any more monsters."

She ground her staff into the box's opening and it collapsed—as though it were simply made out of cardboard.

"Takako, this is fun and all...but how do we get out of here?"

"You need to defeat all the Suits and destroy the boxes, *then* find and defeat the giant Suit."

"How big are we talking?"

I shrugged.

"*Okay,* so where do we *find* the giant Suit?"

"It really depends. It seems like this place is a maze, so who knows how many dead ends we'll run into."

Manami hefted the scepter onto her shoulder. "I'm gonna smash the wall."

"Don't you dare."

"Too late!" And with that—Manami swung her scepter, this time like a baseball bat.

The glassy heart stayed intact...and instead the wall shattered like a black mirror.

A good thing that I ducked.

She pulled the scepter back for another swing, but I raised a placating hand. "Don't!"

"But we have to get to the end of the maze!" Manami pushed through my gesture and prodded at the broken wall, shards twisting and falling away until she was satisfied with a jagged opening large enough for us to crouch through.

"Are you the type to draw a line through dead-ends when completing a maze on paper?"

Manami put a hand on her hip, smirking in admiration of her handiwork. "Not since I was little."

I sighed. "Let's just go. I don't know if the Suits have a psychic connection to this world—they might be able to detect where we are if we destroy stuff."

Manami's eyes widened. "*Oopsie...*"

We stepped over the threshold and found ourselves in a hallway extending who knows how long to the right, and a little bit to the left before going around another corner.

I looked both ways, determining our next course of action as Manami weighed the scepter in her hands—her eagerness to smash through another wall outweighing any and all logic I could come up with.

Sigh. "Okay."

Manami beamed at me and skipped forward, following through with the scepter and making another heroic entrance.

A swarm of Suits hissed at us like rats from the other side of the wall. Manami spun on her toe, ribbon flapping from the momentum—and the monsters disintegrated into nothing, a few leaving behind the usual desserts for me to harvest.

"I guess just keep doing what you're doing." I pointed at the next wall. "Go on, smash it."

She hesitated.

"What?"

"It's just kinda weird, you know?" Manami fiddled with the staff in her hands. "I thought being a magical girl would, like...give me an idea of what to say?"

"What to say?"

"Yeah—like catch phrases and stuff. I thought maybe I'd just *say* it. Like how this outfit just appeared, maybe the words would just *come* to me."

Thinking back to the different entries in *Magical Girl Monthly*...

Were there any catch phrases besides my own transformation speech?

I didn't have time to respond.

At the top of her lungs, Manami shouted, "I will break through all the evil in these monsters' hearts!"

She cocked her hip to the side and gave a peace sign.

These monsters are no match for the power of love—she added, playfully sticking her tongue out and winking.

Must've been practicing that in front of a mirror to get it that perfect.

OO6

Kenji flopped on the ground—still sobbing, but running out of steam.

Torn and crumpled playing cards surrounded him. Some were scorched...others were partially melted, or dissolved in still-bubbling puddles.

"Heyyyy," Miyako said. She pushed aside some of the pointier toys in the pile and sat down, facing away from Kenji. "Are ya done?"

The boy let out a whine that turned into a choked sob. His arms gave the illusion that his face was propped up—but in reality, his face was pressed flat against the dank floor, drool at the corners of his mouth.

Miyako groaned. "You're such a wimp, ya know? You've got this *whole area* to yourself. I'd be *thrilled!*"

"I wanna *leave*," Kenji snarled into the floor.

"Well, you're gonna get your chance *soon*—just gotta be patient."

"Wait! *What?*" He pushed himself off the floor.

"Yeah—*Dad* wanted me to tell you. He's gonna let ya leave soon!" She stood and paced around in the shadows. "Actually, he wanted you to know *earlier!*"

"*What?*"

Miyako cackled. "Ha! Yeah. That's why I came here earlier. I mean, besides givin' you that deck o' cards. Which..." She looked at the aftermath of his tantrum and sighed. "Looks like *that* didn't last long."

Kenji's lip trembled again. "W-Why wouldn't you tell me that I can leave?"

"You were bein' such a twerp," she said, between laughs. "Why would I *reward* that?"

He stood up and stomped his foot.

"Now, now—now you know that you *can* leave. But if you misbehave again, I won't tell you *how* to get out of here. *Ever.*"

"Miyakoooo..." Kenji whined.

"And ya know what? I don't think you're even *ready* to go."

"No! I'm ready! I'm *ready!*" he said, bouncing eagerly.

"Are ya *sure?* I don't think you have enough *power* yet. If ya try now, you're just gonna get hurt."

"I can *do it,* Miyako! Just *tell me!*"

"Eager little puppy, aren't you?" Miyako let out a maniacal titter before stepping forward, the shadows following her, obscuring her so she was just a dark form compared to the rest of the Darkness.

She leaned down—and whispered into Kenji's ear...

OO7

I didn't even have a chance to stand up.

Manami slung her bag over her shoulder and pointed at me with her empty bubble tea cup. In her other hand, she held up her pathetic strip of transformation paper. It waved about—nothing special about it now that there were no monsters to fight, and no reason to transform.

You're gonna explain stuff to me—she had said, and informed me that we were getting coffee.

And *that* was how I found myself sitting outside the coffee shop that I had wanted to go to before the Suits appeared.

It's funny how these things work out.

Manami licked some whipped cream off her upper lip. "So..."

"So?" I reached for my coffee but had second thoughts.

Too much steam—I'd scald my tongue if I took a sip now.

"So, the Suits. They're really just...gone? There's like, no monster that I have to talk to? And teach the power of love and friendship to?"

"Yeah, they're gone."

"The giant Suit wasn't like...someone transformed into a monster? With the smaller ones being...I dunno, a look into their insecurities? Was someone peeved that they couldn't use a coupon on top of the sale? And they threw a chair? Or maybe they had some other issue that amplified everyone else's negativity!"

"I don't know what to tell you, Manami. The monsters we'll be fighting are just that—monsters."

I hope.

I mean, the magazine would tell me if they were people to begin with, right?

"What about that guy over there?" she continued, ignoring me. "Oh, or that girl, there! She goes to our school!"

"Manami, *no one* here is responsible for what happened today. Besides," I scoffed, picking up my black coffee and blowing on it, "we can't just walk up to random strangers on the street and ask for their life stories. Like, what insecurities would even be represented by card suits?"

"Okay, but like...what about that kid over there? He looks like *he's* got problems." Manami gestured at a kid across the street from us. "Oh, never mind. They stopped."

"Stopped?"

"Yeah, they were playing keep away with him. That's why I pointed him out. Really feels like that's something I should've *intervened* in. Y'know...being a *magical girl* and all."

"I guess you could, if that puts you in the mood to fight more monsters."

I looked over at the group of five boys, all huddled around one who was playing on a portable video game system. Maybe the Suits came from their game? Miku *did* say at one point that our powers and the monsters seemed like an RPG.

"Mm... Nah. They'd probably laugh at me if I stepped in now. A high school gal walking over to grade schoolers and telling them what to do...not a *bad* look, but odd, y'know?"

You should really intervene against bullies—magical girl or not— regardless of if they laugh, I murmured.

Another sip of coffee.

It was cold.

Exactly how long had I been staring at them?

Manami reached over the table and held her iced coffee to my forehead.

"*Gah!*" I jolted back. "What was that for?"

160

"Did transforming the both of us like, make you sick or something? You look kinda *glum*."

"I'm *fine*." I prodded her cup out of the way with the back of my hand and took another sip from my cup.

Gag.

Splutter.

"Want me to get you a refill? Cold coffee *sucks* when it's not cold on purpose."

"No, that's fine."

I took a small sip, holding it in my mouth, wanting to avoid swallowing it.

Though that made the taste linger and the texture worse.

Manami got up, pushed her chair in, and said: *That's it—I'm getting you something sweet to cancel out the bad taste.*

She saw I was about to decline, and she glared—swiping my coffee cup from my hands. "I *insist*."

I slouched down in my seat, defeated.

As Manami went back into the shop, I decided to look back across the street. The boys were still there—roughhousing again as she said they had been.

Fighting over the gaming system, to be specific.

My wrought iron chair scraped the sidewalk, maybe fast enough to create sparks, and called out, *Oi!*

Loud enough to turn heads at the other tables, but not loud enough for the boys to hear.

I stood there for a moment, marinating in that awkwardness, before slowly sitting back down.

I want to bury my face in my arms, but people would stare.

No, people are *already* staring.

I want to leave, but...

"I'm baa-aack!" Manami sang as she sat down and pressed a cold cup into my hand. "I know you're always bringing flan to school, and seeing all the pudding and flan during the battle got me thinking about it—so I got you a caramel iced coffee with whipped cream and a chocolate drizzle!"

"Oh." I blinked and refocused, looking at the drink I now held.

It was excessive compared to my usual order, to say the least.

"Thanks."

"*Soooo...*" Manami drew out the word and tilted her head.

She hadn't released the drink, arm still outstretched—just like the syllable.

So there *is* a price to her kindness.

"I'm *obviously* not the first magical girl in town."

"Right..." Where's she going with this?

"So like..." Manami leaned further forward, negating the fact that she had sat down across from me. "Are the others from our school?"

I realized she had yet to provide me with a straw. "What do *you* think?" I asked, leaning forward to lick the tip of the whipped cream.

Manami probably realized I wasn't going to give information up this easily, so she relented and passed me a straw. I unwrapped it and stuck it in my drink. She crossed her arms and pursed her lips as she thought about her answer. "Well, probably not. That'd be kinda *dumb* on your part." She tilted her head. "No offense."

"No, it's all right. You're right that it wouldn't be the smartest move."

And yet...

She hit the bullseye.

"Yeah, but then again, it wouldn't be expected. And like, the first three battles happened at school. It'd make sense for the *other* girls to go there, too. Then again, who's to say you were behind the others?"

"Mm."

She leaned back into her chair and crossed her legs. "I'm not gonna get *any* answers from you today—*am* I?"

I stared at her, furrowing my brows ever so slightly. "You're not *ready* for my answers."

Mainly because even *I* don't know.

"Hm, I guess not. In all the shows I used to watch, the mascots wouldn't tell the girls everything at first. They'd just be like, 'Nya! *You* deal with all your studies and stuff, while *I* just go and do some other stuff—narrow down our search for the *princess,* et cetera.'" Manami slurped her iced coffee. "Never made sense to me. They should've realized that it was the *first* magical girl who was the princess. Looked exactly like her, too—*unless* that similarity was just for the audience's sake."

"A princess?"

"Yeah!" She slid the straw in and out a couple times, making that grating sound of plastic on plastic, pushing the ice cubes around, before stopping suddenly and looking up at me. "Takako...am *I* a princess?"

"Uh..."

"Come on, you *have* to break the pattern! Like, just tell me up front! Are you *looking* for someone? Do I look like her?"

"Well, I *am* looking for someone. I think." I drank some of my coffee. "Don't know if she's a princess, though."

"Ooh, *cool!* Is that why you transferred to Fujioka High?"

I sighed. "I have to be real with you, Manami."

"Oh?"

"I woke up last month on a sofa with no memory of who I was—or how I got there."

"*So*...what you're *saying* is..." Manami's pink eyes sparkled as she looked at me, intensely. "*You're* the princess!"

"How did you get that from—"

"Because it's *unexpected!* It like...breaks away from the mold! You think the person you're looking for has all the answers, but really the answers were inside of *you.*" She slurped her coffee. "Who're you lookin' for, anyway?"

"I don't..."

"Listen! I can keep an eye out."

Sigh. "I don't know her name, or her face. She has long, light brown hair that kinda looks like a cloud."

"A cloud?"

"Very fluffy." I put my drink down and held my hands up. "It looked like it moved on its own?"

"Do you know what she'd be wearing?"

I held my chin in my hand.

The lighting was always dim in my dream, and I never thought about what she was wearing, but...

"Pink. She wore a pink dress. And..." I pointed at the side of my head, opposite the curl that never stays down. "I think she had a bow on this side?"

"*Cute!* Anything else you remember?"

"She loves flan—but thinks very highly of it?"

"Huh?"

"You know how you can go into any convenience store and get a cup of flan? She made it seem like flan is something more for special occasions—that vanilla and chocolate pudding are what's common."

"So she's American. Got it!"

I hadn't noticed, but Manami had been typing on her phone—with one hand, under the table. "What are you doing?"

"Makin' a thread. I'll let you know what the responses are when I get some." She swiped at the screen with her thumb and pressed the button to post it.

"Oh, you didn't have to!"

"Of *course* I did!" She slammed her drink down on the table. "You deserve to find happiness with your princess! Live the magical girl dream, Takako!"

I was about to thank her, when a playful jingle interrupted me.

"Oh, *crap!*" Manami looked at her phone screen—black with pink accents—as it continued to jingle. Then to her wristwatch. "I should've been home by now!" She hoisted her bag over her shoulder and grabbed her empty cup to throw away. "I'll see you around, Takako! Bye bye!"

I blinked and took out my own phone.

It *was* late. The sun would be setting soon.

Where did the time go?

I shifted my bag into my lap, dipping my fingers in.

Magical Girl Monthly had yet again vanished from my bag.

008

"Gorgeous. You brought a Magical Tutorial Goddess here? Are you *daft?*"

"Hey, I can explain—"

"I have never doubted you." The woman flipped her hair indignantly, before her posture straightened.

It's all right—Gorgeous didn't mean to upset us, my children, she added in a hushed tone, looking at the back of her shoulder.

Gorgeous and her companion were a shadow puppet presentation for the audience—silhouettes behind a curtain at Suzu's bedside.

Suzu stirred from her slumber, sitting up and rubbing sand from her eye.

"Oh, *look* who's awake." The curtain swished open, and the mystery woman glared at Suzu with her pale-yellow eyes. "Brat."

"I didn't *ask* to be brought here!"

"Of course. No one ever does. We often find ourselves at an impasse in our lives, and either step aside to let others through or stand there, dumbfounded—stopping the self-improvement of others."

"I don't get it..."

Me neither.

"Does anyone really 'get' it if there's nothing physical to obtain? No one 'gets' knowledge—it is provided and absorbed, or seen and dismissed. No one 'gets' it, as it's not something physical that only one person can own. It may be considered a gift to some—but it never fully leaves the hands of the one who gives it."

The woman sat down on the bed, adjusting the fabric of her green and blue negligee and fixing her ornate headdress that rested atop her long, straight hair the color of a midnight sky.

"*Bewitching*." She held out a hand. Something small with many legs scuttled between her fingers. "*Charmed* to make your acquaintance."

Suzu did not take her hand. Instead, she stared into space as she processed the monologue.

Brat—Bewitching spat at her again, then turned to Gorgeous. "*Clearly* she isn't ready to join us, if she isn't even able to feign politeness."

"She's seen the state Elegant is in." Gorgeous scowled. "She's ready."

"Ah—you didn't *start* with that. How was I to know?" Bewitching cradled her chin in her palm. She repeated: *How were we supposed to know?*

"I thought one of your little *friends* would have told you." Gorgeous crossed her arms. "As per *usual*."

"True, true. *Nothing* can escape our knowledge for long. We will *always* find out...but that is still no excuse to intentionally withhold information from us."

"God, you're creepy."

"And yet—you don't avert your gaze."

Suzu broke her silence. "You're the Bug Mother—Bringer of Calamity."

"Oh, is *that* what they're calling me?"

The *Bug Mother?*

Was she a villain from the previous season?

Her powers seem fitting to be those of a villain—the unsettling aspect of having bugs constantly crawling on your skin by choice...

I shivered.

Judging by the established naming scheme, Bewitching was obviously a former Tutorial Goddess.

But why is the side of the Tutorial Goddesses *bad,* and the Deadly Omen Finders are *good?*

Then there's also the matter of her *other* title...

"We can't choose the powers we're given, Suzu..." Gorgeous explained. "And we can't help that they always end up being gilded."

"Gilded?" Suzu asked.

"Haven't you noticed? You encounter technology everywhere in your everyday life—and your powers come from it. How would you feel right now if I took away your precious headphones?" Gorgeous asked, gesturing to them.

Suzu instinctively reached for them, and relaxed when she found them still around her neck. "You didn't take them off earlier? Even though I was asleep?"

"Well, do *you* take them off for bed?"

No response.

"That's what I thought. Every time I've seen you out of your transformation—don't look at me like that—you've been wearing them. And now the truth comes out that you never take them off—even when you sleep."

"I only wear them to bed after a long battle..."

"But you *admit* to having done it."

Bewitching sighed. "You need to get to the point faster, Gorgeous."

"Do *you* want to explain it to her?"

Bewitching smirked. "Would you like to know why I'm crawling with bugs? It's the same reason why you need to be in contact with technology, and why Elegant is near death."

Suzu gripped at the ear cups. "*Why?*"

"It's great to be able to control something, isn't it? However, we were never in control of our powers. That's simply what they *wanted* us to believe."

"When we're transformed, our powers have a *positive* effect. We each have our own dominion. But for us to control our powers," Gorgeous explained, "the Elves let us know through the power of suggestion that we need to surround ourselves with whatever our dominion is. We need to be in our *element*. Hence, you wear your headphones, Bewitching has her insects, and my little sister had to be placed in stasis."

Makes sense...

"Eventually, we become so powerful that our powers have a *negative* effect when not transformed. It consumes us. Omens are created."

"Goddesses...become Omens?"

"No. Haven't you been listening? Your power gains a life of its own—breaking away from you. When you can no longer control it, your power attacks *you*. And *that* is the Omen."

"B-But what's Elegant's power?"

"My sister is able to control spirits...but they started to get violent when she wasn't transformed. It was because she had so much *life*—she lost control of her powers over *death*. When she's in this state, she's close enough to being dead that they don't bother her, or anyone in the area. If an Omen is created from her powers...it'll result in a mass-extinction event."

Gorgeous crossed her arms and looked in the direction of the tube, currently unlit.

"Sometimes she'll appear as a spirit and wander around this room," Bewitching explained, "but she can't see or hear anyone here. It's not the same as having her around."

Gorgeous covered her mouth, trying to choke back a sob and failing. "She was so *lively,* and I miss her *so much.*"

Will there be negative side effects to the powers I'm giving my classmates?

Will plants start growing from Nana's fingers?

Will Youko's lungs fill with water?

Will Hotaru develop pyrokinesis?

Will Manami become the target of a multitude of stalkers?

I'm just *creating* magical girls—but still transforming to gift them their powers.

What would *my* side effect be?

Will I turn into an animal mascot, more fitting for an anime than real life?

No—*Magical Girl Monthly* hasn't said anything about side effects...

And I'm probably over-thinking all of this. Who said these *theoretical* side effects have to be *bad?*

If there are side effects when we're not transformed, they could be beneficial—we could have complete control over our powers and use them to help the world in a wider variety of ways!

Wishful thinking.

Regardless, I couldn't bear to watch the rest of the episode so I walked up to the TV and turned it off—the remote still eluding me—and I went to bed, wishing for the next battle to turn out all right.

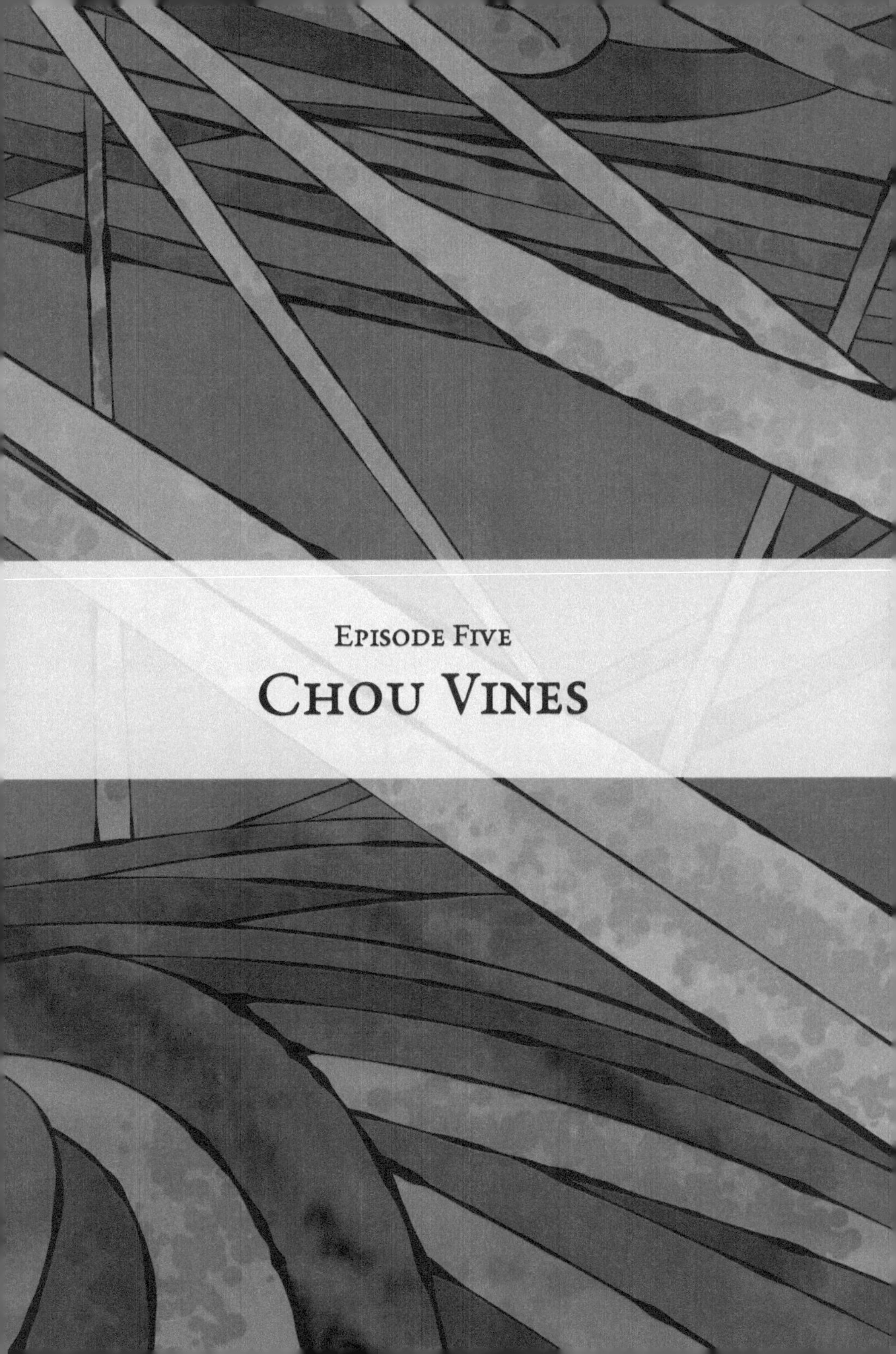

Episode Five

Chou Vines

OOI

"That was so *cool!*" Tsubasa exclaimed, holding my hands. "The first three girls' powers were elemental, so they'd probably be the easiest to fake. But the power of *love?* There's no faking *that!*"

Masuyo and Miku walked over to my desk.

"I *knew* it had to be something paranormal!" Masuyo exclaimed, turning to face the rest of the class. "*None* of you would believe me! But *I* was *right!*"

No one turned to face the countenance that just *beamed* with the joy of vindication.

I still think it's special effects—Miku replied. She took off her glasses and cleaned them with the hem of her hoodie. "Virtual reality. Augmented reality. Holograms." Placing her glasses back on her nose, she added, *I mean, technology is advancing. It could be something that we've never seen before.*

"Yeah," Tsubasa drawled. "None of us have seen magical girls before—thought that was obvious."

Miku adjusted her glasses' position and sighed, trying to ignore her. "Besides, the *elemental* attacks seem like the easiest to fake? Of course, they could be using practical effects for those—but *love?* Isn't it more obvious that *that* would be the easiest to fake? Just take a projector or pink lights, angle everything just right—or even edit it in post, really, since no witnesses ever come forward—and *presto!* You've got the fake 'power of love.' Heck, this girl's weapon was a giant *lollipop*. Feels like it's foreshadowing that *you're* all gonna turn out to be the *suckers* in this situation if you keep on believing this."

Tsubasa crossed her arms. "I don't think it's paranormal abilities—*or* special effects, *or* practical effects!"

"What is it, then?" I asked.

Tsubasa beamed at my inquiry, confidently puffing out her chest and resting her fists on her hips—a power stance. "Aliens, of course!"

Masuyo clapped their hands together once. "That *is* paranormal! So you really *do* agree with me!"

Tsubasa crossed her arms and *tsk*ed, shaking her head. "I never should've left the Paranormal Club."

She walked forward, and Masuyo backed into a desk.

Nose to nose, Tsubasa announced, "Aliens are *real*. There's a lot of evidence of *extraterrestrial* life on other planets, Masuyo! Don't lump them in because *you* have doubts!"

Masuyo relaxed as Tsubasa took a step back, but jumped when she made a grand gesture with outstretched arms.

"If you discovered a weird-looking, deep-sea *fish*...or some sorta cave-dwelling *creature*...or a *plant* that grows only on the highest mountain peak or in the deepest part of a forest—you wouldn't say, *Oh, that's paranormal!* You'd think, *Oh, this is something that science has yet to encounter and fully explore!*" Tsubasa pointed at Masuyo's nose. "Same thing with aliens!"

"Actually," Miku said, looking down at her phone, "aliens *are* considered paranormal."

She must have had an article bookmarked for this very occasion.

Her preparedness is a bit off-putting.

You're wrong—Tsubasa interjected.

Miku blinked. "I have multiple sources that say otherwise."

Just how prepared *is* she?

"*They're* wrong!" Tsubasa interjected once again.

"In that case, what are *your* sources?" Miku asked, opening a new tab in preparation to type in whatever site Tsubasa would supply.

174

"Hm?" Tsubasa's demeanor completely changed, her light voice becoming dark.

Tsubasa...are you not Flan Girl, but the *villain* in this story?

"You *really* want to know?"

"Uh...yeah?" the bespectacled girl replied. "That's *kinda* why I asked?"

Tsubasa reached up and pointed her finger to the heavens—and her demeanor changed back, stars forming in her eyes.

"The *aliens,* of course!"

"The..." Miku's thumb hovered over her keyboard as she looked up. "The aliens?"

"Yeah, yeah!" Tsubasa exclaimed, pointing at the girl with both her index fingers, excited from the response her announcement garnered. "They came to me last month—the night before the semester started! When I was watching the shooting stars! And, and, *and*—they said they didn't appreciate being lumped in with ghosts, psychics, demons, and the like!"

"The like..." Miku locked her phone. I half-expected smoke to start issuing from her overloaded brain.

My attention was then drawn to Tsubasa.

All that energy...

She's so much like Flan Girl.

I'm sorry, Tsubasa!

I take back what I thought about you being the villain!

Please forgive me!

"Are you *sure* you weren't dreaming?" Masuyo asked with some hesitation in their voice.

"Positive."

"One time, I had a dream, and in it I asked my dad if I was dreaming." Miku paused to build suspense, drawing everyone's attention to her. "He lied to me."

OO2

Kenji sat alone in the Darkness—bored out of his mind, with nothing to do. He'd even pulled out a few strands of hair from his head to play with in the three ways he could think of—wrapping them around his fingers until they were numb, flossing his recently erupted teeth, and splitting them on his axe until they couldn't be split anymore. They would fade away, back into the Darkness for him to one day reabsorb. His body had been created from the Darkness, so there was no wonder it didn't dull his senses—this room, to some extent, was an extension of his being, as was the case for all of his family.

So, when he felt a presence behind him, he immediately stood at attention.

"What'd you bring me?" Kenji held out his hands, expectantly.

Miyako stood just out of his line of sight, tapping her foot. "Hm, what *did* I bring my *darlin'* little *bother?*" she asked, dragging out Kenji's anticipation. "Isn't it possible I'm just *visitin'?*" Her hands remained behind her back as she orbited Kenji's little play area, not revealing whether the only thing she held was a bluff.

"Come *onnnn!*" Kenji whined, stamping his feet, all the while living up to his nickname.

"Kay!" Miyako cheered. "But—ya gotta pick a hand!" She shrugged her left shoulder. "One has a gift..." She shrugged her right. "And the other..." She cackled.

"What? What is it?" Kenji vibrated with excitement.

"It's a *surprise!*" Miyako made a show of shuffling the contents of her hands back and forth. "You're just gonna have to pick the hand that has it if ya ever wanna find out! One time deal, y'know?"

"Uh...um..." Kenji ran his fingers through his hair. "W-Which do I pick? Which do I pick?"

"Y'need a *hint?*"

"No! I choose..." He fidgeted. "This one!" He pointed at the hand on his right, Miyako's left.

"*Da* da-da *daaaa~*" Miyako whipped her hand up into the air, flourishing a bouquet of dandelions that was in no way small enough for her to have hidden it behind her.

"Is that the gift? Or the surprise?"

"Let's see..." Miyako lowered her hand and rotated her wrist, examining the bouquet. "*Is* it the gift? Or the *surprise?*"

Kenji—no longer caring for her hemming and hawing—made grabby hands again. "Gimme!"

"Kay!" Miyako turned around and tossed the bouquet over her shoulder—her other hand was empty.

The boy caught it more with his chest and upper arms than with his hands, and fumbled to get a better grip on it.

"*Anyway,*" Miyako said as she walked away, "you're gonna need to get used to different senses from outside."

Kenji beamed. "Outside?"

No response.

He plopped himself down on the ground and tossed the plant life above him. Seeds and dust and pollen flew into the air as the weeds fell back into his lap.

Kenji rubbed the stems between his fingers, squeezing goo out and rubbing it all over his hands. He wrapped the stems around his fingers, but they just didn't allow for the same amount of pressure as the strands of his hair had.

They were *also* far too thick and bitter tasting to floss with.

Kenji brought his hands up and wiped his face.

It was always a neutral temperature in the Darkness, but the dewy texture felt cool against his skin.

And then it felt prickly and hot.

Kenji covered his face, sneezing forcefully into his palms. Once again, he grasped the dandelions—this time gripping them by the flowers and seeds.

The powder coated his hands like the ashes from his matches had not that long ago. It mixed with his snot in a horrible mess...which he tried to wipe on his shirt.

He sneezed again.

OO3

The rest of the school day was uneventful, and I soon found myself walking out the gates. To some extent, I'd given up my experiments of testing when the magazine disappears.

Will a battle happen soon? Yes.

Do I have the magazine on my person? To my knowledge, yes.

I zoned out, thinking about where the next monsters would appear.

Of course, I wasn't tuning my surroundings out completely.

After all—I saw Chou.

She was on her hands and knees, on the edge of the sidewalk—definitely a tripping hazard.

I stopped and stood there for a moment, wondering how I could get her attention, before deciding to ask the classic: *What are you doing?*

Chou jolted, and quickly got into a crouch. "Oh! Tako! Good to see you!" She waved her hands in an attempt to remove suspicion...but this did nothing to hide the fact that they were speckled with bits of dirt and gravel.

I decided not to comment on it. "*Tako?*"

"Yeah!" Chou *glomp*ed me, though I was able to resist the power of a full tackle and stayed upright. She's the shortest girl in my class, but stronger than she looks. "Your name is *Takako!* So I shortened it to *Tako,* 'cause your hair reminds me of an *octopus!*"

She released me from her grasp and started picking the gravel from her knees and palms—then looked up at me, only to be met with my confusion.

"It's cute, *nya!* And octopus and fish are *delish!*"

"Moving on..." Not a fan of the nickname. I'm too tired for this. Can we just get this whole thing over with? *Please?* "Why are you crawling around outside the school? You're gonna get tripped over."

"Well, ya see...it's like this..." Chou rubbed her cheeks with the backs of her hands, as if to groom herself. "I'm a *cat,* nya!"

I nodded.

Normally, this is where anyone else would walk away. But of course, *Magical Girl Monthly* said today's monster *needed* to be defeated by Chou, so...

"A *demon* cat, nya!"

My bag fell off my shoulder. "Come again?"

"My bow is *really* a talisman that keeps my powers in check!" Chou jumped up, her hands in the air with her fingers curled into her palms. She bumped her hip to the side, imitating a swishing tail. "Y'know, *'nya'?*"

Her biography in the magazine *did* mention she was *chuuni...*

"So, you're on all fours outside the school...because you're a cat demon?"

"Yes!" Chou cheered, enthusiastically pumping her fist in the air. "Wait, no." She paused, gasped, and got back on her knees. Looking under the hedge that ran alongside the wall, she held out her hand, making comforting and beckoning sounds.

It was then that Aki and her entourage approached.

"*Oh* ho *ho,* would you look at *that?* The *chuuni* is alone today—no *gal* in sight."

That's right—Manami ended up leaving school early today because she was feeling under the weather. Usually, she probably walks with Chou until they part ways.

Chou focused all her attention on the shadows under the bush, and either didn't notice Aki's condescending clique or pretended not to.

I glared at them in her stead.

Aki's gaze shifted to me, and she rested a hand on her hip. "Oh, it's *Flan* Girl."

"Flan Girl is my...*friend*. I'm..." I scowled. "*Tako.*"

Aki's eyebrows and upper lip started to twitch, and she raised her hand in readiness to cover her laugh.

Wow, it must be a big one.

Instead, she brought her elbow up to her nose and sneezed.

Hikari dug into her bag and took out a lacy handkerchief. She passed it to Aki, who snatched it wordlessly.

Hikari then sneezed, followed by Yukiko.

"Oh, are you all *catching* something?" Aoi asked. She reached into her own bag, taking out disposable face masks and passing them out.

No, Yukiko replied—before sneezing again and gladly accepting the mask.

"Someone's—*obviously*—talking a-a-about—me!" Aki announced between rapid-fire sneezes.

"Why aren't *you* sneezing?" Hikari asked.

"*I* remembered to take my *allergy medication* this morning." Aoi smirked, steepling her fingers. "*Nothing* will faze me," she said—before succumbing to a sneeze, jumping backwards from the force. She took out a mask of her own—thick fabric, embroidered with her name—and put it on.

"Well, you four should *probably* get going," I suggested. "You don't want to get even *more* sick."

"*You* don't tell *me* what to—"

"You're right!" Aoi bounced in front of Aki, cutting her off. "Come on, we need to go into quarantine!"

The group moved on—Aoi skipping in the lead, occasionally sneezing and jumping back a few paces.

I squatted down to look at the receiving end of Chou's attention. "So, is there a cat under there or something?"

Chou perked up after seemingly blocking out the entire exchange I had with Aki and the others. "Nya!"

"I'll take that as a 'yes!'"

A silver cat with stripes darted out from underneath.

"Kitty!"

The cat hissed at Chou before running away as fast as its little paws could carry it.

Chou pouted. "That *never* happens. Kitties *love* me. Something must've *spooked* it."

The hedge's leaves shook in a non-existent wind—and they turned to face us.

"W-What—"

I grabbed Chou's sleeve. "Just grab your bag and *slowly* walk away."

She did as she was told and followed me back through the school's gates. We neared the entrance of the main building. A few lingering students and clubs were engrossed in their activities, and I noted they had yet to be affected.

"S-So..." Chou trembled. "Where are we going?"

"Back to the classroom." Not really. "I forgot something." Not really.

"Are...are we not gonna talk about the—"

"Just wait a minute."

"W-Wait a minute?"

"All right—maybe a little *longer* than a minute."

I continued to lead the way up the winding stairs, through the halls. Chou paused outside the classroom, expecting me to go in—but I didn't hesitate to walk past it.

I unzipped my bag a little bit.

Magical Girl Monthly was still there.

Good.

At the top of the final stairwell, I opened the heavy door and let Chou through to the roof first.

"What are we doing up here?"

"Look down."

Chou looked over the guard rail.

More plants came to life, spitting their spores into the air. None of them should reach us up here, unless there's a large gust of wind—but even then, I doubt we would be affected by it, since we're going to transform soon enough.

"See all of this chaos?" I gestured to the track next to the gym behind the school, where Nana, Hotaru, and the rest of whatever sports team were collapsing one after another from non-stop sneezing. "It's targeting our classmates, everyone in school—and it's spreading to the town. But *you* can—"

"*Kitty!*" Chou ran and grasped the railing, squealing, bouncing up and down as she saw the cat from earlier. It stretched before curling up on the wall that ran the school's perimeter, no longer worried about the ongoing disaster.

"N-No?" I gestured once again to all the students. "Are...are you *really* not seeing everyone succumbing to bad allergies?"

"I'm nearsighted!"

"That...that makes absolutely *no sense* whatsoever!"

"*Cat*-sighted, nya!" Chou corrected herself. "If there's a kitty nearby, my eyes jump to it!"

Frustrated, I grabbed her by the shoulder and turned her around. "You have the *power* to *fix* this."

"Nya?"

"Here, just...let me show you."

I flipped to Chou's page in the magazine and tore out a paper strip—it was yellow, orange, and brown, a jumble of paw prints that from a distance looked like furry blobs. Instead of handing it to her, I reached out and patted her head with it.

"There you go."

Chou blinked her big brown eyes up at me.

"I, Takako, take this task of delivering justice to this evil in the form of another hero. Yadda yadda *yadda*... I, Takako, now sleep as I wear this mask and my true power awakens!"

After a rushed transformation, I looked over to Chou, who ogled her new outfit and—more importantly—new appendage.

"I...I have a *tail,* nya!" She spun around, trying to catch the brunette tail. She wore a brown, asymmetrical crop top, and a short yellow skirt that bore a single, large, brown paw print. Both seemed to have a rough, fur-like texture to the fabric. She had brown, furry wristbands and anklets, and a spiked cat collar. She still had the yellow baubles in her pigtails.

"And ears," I added. "Well, I mean, you had ears before. What I mean is, you have *cat* ears now. And yellow cat eyes."

The cat girl reached up and pet her ears, jolting back as they twitched to the touch.

Before she could push back her hair and find out if her human ears were still intact—a philosophical question about cat girls that I'm not ready to find out the answer for—I swatted her hands away, stirring her from her reverie.

"Tako!" Chou looked up at me with shining eyes. "Am I a *pretty* kitty?"

"We'll get you a mirror later so you can decide that for yourself. Right now, you have to fight."

"Oh, okay!" She leapt over the balcony as I was in mid-kneel.

"W-Wait!" I stood and gripped the balcony, watching Chou land on all fours. "You can't just...*aargh!*" I followed her down.

"So, who do I have to fight?"

"Chou, *please,* just *listen,* you—"

"I hope it's Fujioka."

"Wait, *what?*"

"She deserves it, *nya!*"

Okay, so while I *may* have to agree with you on that one... "You have to use your powers against the *real* evil that's happening around us right now!"

"*Fine,*" Chou huffed.

I looked around, making sure no one had seen us. All of the students were writhing on the ground, sneezing and coughing. "If you were to fight in this world, you'd cause collateral damage." I knelt down. "Go through the portal. Fight there."

"What portal—*ohhh!*"

And with that, Chou got on all fours and pounced through the torn curtain of space.

OO4

Chou's ears twitched, her tail swishing behind her as she looked on at the Vines that sprouted from untamed flower beds.

I didn't get a chance to call out orders—when she crouched down, pounced forward, and grabbed onto the nearest Vine, sinking her claws and teeth into it.

The leaves on the surrounding Vines shook again in a non-existent wind. The thinner Vines formed a lattice wall between me and Chou, while the thicker ones snaked below her feet in a spiral as she continued to *nom* on her Vine of choice.

"Chou! Get out of there!"

She finally released the Vine from her fangs with a *pah!* "Huh? What'd ya say, Tako?"

The bite marks shrank until the Vine was smooth again—as though Chou had never gnawed on it.

She looked over to me through the barrier, then retracted her claws from the Vine.

Once again, the Vine regenerated, and the one step she took towards me—

It was a mistake.

The thick Vines surrounding her writhed—she had activated a snare.

One Vine wrapped around her leg, yanking her into the air and flinging her at the wall. The other Vines tangled loosely around her.

The wall between us stretched into a dome.

A cage.

It wound around again and again, thoroughly covering any gaps.

Covering any possible exit.

"Tako!" Chou screamed through sobs and sneezes. She reached for me through a gap in the cage. "H-Help me!"

I rushed forward, hand outstretched—millimeters away from touching her fingertips.

A Vine snaked up her arm, and yanked her to the center of the cage.

The plants released their spores all at once, engulfing her in a yellow cloud.

I turned away as the pollen blew past me, ducking down and covering my nose and mouth so I wouldn't succumb to debilitating allergies as everyone else had.

My hair and clothes shook in the shock wave.

I waited for everything to be still—then waited an extra few seconds to be absolutely sure I wouldn't be the next target—before looking up.

I looked up.

The Vines slowly receded from their formation, back to how they were when we entered the Green World...and Chou was gone.

Not literally, but figuratively.

For the first time as a spectator to one of these battles, I felt absolutely helpless.

How are we going to get out of here if Chou can no longer fight?

Wait...

Something...is in my right hand.

I held out my hand, palm up and fingers open.

No, nothing is there that I can see, but I can still *feel* a cold weight— and it's slowly getting heavier.

I enclosed my fingers around the metal as it became visible. It extended in two directions from my hand, becoming a long staff, though its weight plateaued. The staff ended in a point to my left, and to my right, it ended with a sphere. I turned my wrist and rested the spike on the ground.

"Well, that's...that's *new*—*oh my God!*"

A curved, obsidian blade grew out of the staff, right below the sphere. Had I been holding the staff any differently, the blade would've split the ends of my hair.

I asked the scythe: *What now?*

As though it would answer my question.

Either my quiet words or the sudden appearance of a magical object drew the Vines' attention to me.

Pushing aside the possibility that *I'm* the *Grim Reaper* of *magical girls*—I firmly grasped the scythe in both hands and clenched my eyes shut.

I swiped it through the air.

Everything was quiet.

I opened my eyes.

In that single swipe, all of the flower beds disappeared—replaced by four-packs of chocolate and vanilla pudding—despite the fact that they were not even in my range.

I swiped the scythe in the other direction, and all of the other Vines disintegrated—replaced with pudding and flan.

One last time, I swiped my scythe through the air...and all of the desserts on the battlefield disappeared, most likely sent to the pudding dimension.

I looked up at the blade in awe.

Seriously—why can't *I* just transform and fight the monsters myself?

Then, I remembered *why* I was able to defeat the monsters single-handedly this time around.

"*Chou!*"

I turned around to face the direction of her defeat...but there was no trace of her.

The Green World faded around me—no door appeared—and I was back on the school grounds, in my school uniform, standing where I had been before opening the portal.

Some students were still sneezing and coughing, but to a lesser extent—*definitely* due to allergies and *not* the monsters.

Chou was still nowhere in sight.

OO5

The next day, Chou was missing from school.

And on Monday, her seat—front row, second from the door—was empty.

This is all *my fault.*

If only I had experimented with or went against the magazine's instructions to put Chou on the front lines.

Maybe someone *else* would have done better against the Vines?

I should've explained the situation to her better before giving her powers.

She was so eager to fight. She went in blindly...and I couldn't stop her.

Manami walked into the classroom through the front door, dark circles under her eyes. Is she still exhausted from her battle against the Suits? Or has she been staying up late, thinking about Chou's disappearance?

Probably both.

She paused to take a look at Chou's empty desk with her own empty eyes.

Manami—a hollow version of herself—slumped down in her own seat, resting her head on her arms.

"See what happened to her for being so *immature?*" Aki called out loudly in her assigned seat next to Manami's. She had just paused an unrelated conversation with Hikari, so it was obvious she was saying this to be a thorn in Manami's side. "Somebody in a dark alley *probably* promised a *cat* to her after school—and then they *abducted* her."

Manami made no move to sit up and argue against the speculation.

In fact, her shoulders shifted as she slouched down in her seat, burying her face further.

Before I could stand and make my way over to the rich girl and tell her to *Show some respect,* a teal blur rushed at her from the back row.

Hikari hustled to Aki's side, who was now on the floor.

"Y-*You!*" Aki exclaimed, holding her face with one hand and pointing up at Miku with the other. "You *punched* my *perfect* cheekbone!"

Miku held her chin aloft. "You're *so* over-dramatic—falling out of your chair *on purpose* from just a slap! If I hit you as hard as you claim, you would've fallen in the other direction—physics aren't something you can *pay* your way out of." She walked back to her seat.

With everyone silently gawking at Aki, I could hear Miku mutter: *Rich bitch.*

Hikari—finally managing to pry Aki's hand away from her cheek to inspect the damage—said, "Well, you're not bleeding or anything. Thank goodness." She looked a little closer, cradling the girl's face in her hand. "It *is* a little pink, though, but I think that's to be expected."

This amateur medical examination got the attention of Aoi as she walked into the classroom. She *zoomed* to the two girls on the floor and leaned in, closely. "*Ooh,* that might leave a *bruise!*"

"Aoi, are you saying that because it will *actually* leave a bruise, or because you *want* it to leave a bruise?" Yukiko asked, following close behind.

Aoi's pink curls bounced about as she whipped around and exclaimed: *Yes!*

Yes to both?

Aki whined, "I, for one, *don't* want to have an *ugly* bruise on my *beautiful* face!" Then, she put on an elitist air—lifting her arm for Hikari to help her up. "Hikari! Escort me to the infirmary! I need my *imported* ice!"

At the mention of the nurse's office, Aoi followed a bit too eagerly, and Yukiko tailed her to make sure she wouldn't cause any mischief.

OO6

Kenji flopped back in his pile of toys, twirling a final yellow dandelion between his index finger and thumb.

It was strange—usually some unseen force would destroy his *special* toys as he was playing with them.

But these dandelions—aside from the destruction caused by his own hands—were perfectly fine.

"Huh."

"What's 'huh'?" Miyako asked out of nowhere.

Kenji held up the dandelion.

"Well...*shit!* Congrats, bro! You managed to not break your toy this time around!"

"*I* don't break my toys!" he snapped.

"Uh, *yeah.* Ya *do.*" Miyako held up a thumb. "You shattered marbles with your axe." Index. "Got your blood on the matches." Middle. "Don't know *how* ya melted the friggin' nozzle on your snow cone machine...but you did." Ring. "And I *saw* you throw your cards around like crazy. Somehow melted those, too."

"I did *not!*" Kenji dug his nails into the stem. "I threw the cards, but someone else melted them!" He pouted. "Same with everything else. Not my fault..."

"Oh...really, now? Whose fault was it, then?"

"Don't know..."

"Exactly! *Excuses,* excuses!"

"Where're Katsurou and Mother?" He looked up at Miyako in the dark. "Or Father?"

"Lookin' for the Stardust."

Kenji's eyes lit up and he stood. "*Stardust?* Can *I* help? I wanna help!"

"You're helpin' by stayin' here—out of our way."

"No!" He stumbled over the pile of toys to Miyako. "I wanna go with *you!* Let me help you look, *please?* It's like hide-and-seek, right? Or a scavenger hunt! It sounds *fun!* I wanna join!"

"Kinda." She rocked on her heels and tilted her head. "You wouldn't like it."

"Why not?"

"Not gonna lie, but it's pretty boring—a version for the grown-ups, y'know? As soon as I bring you with me, you'll just wanna come back here."

Like the last time you joined us on the hunt—she added, under her breath.

"Oh..." Kenji's shoulders sagged. "Why don't I remember last time?"

"Ignore that—I was dumb and said the wrong thing. It happens. I'm allowed."

Kenji looked down and sniffled, avoiding her gaze.

Miyako crouched, heels on the ground, arms outstretched. "Hey. C'mere, you."

Kenji took a few steps forward, accepting her embrace.

"You get to have the most fun out of all of us by staying here...y'know that, Ken-Ken? I *wish* I could spend all day lazing about. You wanna use *all* this time that you've got to the *fullest*—playin' with your toys. *Not* huntin' for Stardust with the rest of us."

Okay—Kenji muttered into the crook of her neck.

Miyako gave one last squeeze—so tight that Kenji had to push her away—before standing and disappearing into the Darkness.

It was only after she left that Kenji realized his dandelion was gone.

007

On the roof, I decided to read *Magical Girl Monthly* cover to cover.

At this point, I'd already read all the biographies. Some parts I memorized—which *definitely wasn't* weird at all, and wasn't on purpose. If I *could,* I would *forget* the facts I learned.

They were like a song that I couldn't remember the last chords to, so my mental CD player kept getting caught on that one note.

Each biography had a fancy border, from which I would tear off a strip of paper to transform a magical girl. They seemed to be color-coded for the most part.

I thought about what Manami had said: *What happens if a strip is lost to the mundane battle of housework?*

Hopefully these papers could get upgraded to actual talismans in the future.

Something like that—a chunky, plastic trinket—would be harder to lose.

The next section had the list of *monsters.*

This magazine is strange—it's thick, but no matter how many times I flip through, the pages don't seem to add up to what they should. Plus, I can't turn to an upcoming monster's page until it's almost time to battle!

And it's not like the pages are stuck together—if I just open the magazine to the last pages, not reading through in a linear fashion, the pages are blank.

As if there is something that *really* doesn't want me to know that far into the future and refuses to let those pages be revealed.

I've thought about it before, but still haven't gotten an answer—what happens if a battle falls on a weekend?

Will the magazine suddenly appear in my apartment, or if I'm wandering about, will it suddenly appear in my grasp?

What if the next magical girl is busy?

It would be easier if they already knew the secret—I could just call them and say: *Hey, I need you to fight a monster tonight.*

But if it's their first time and we didn't talk at all before then...

I flipped through the pages quickly from start to finish—but this time, there was another section at the end instead of just blank pages.

Revival.

The instructions are vague—*very* vague.

The flan I've been collecting during battles...

A specific time frame...

Some sort of ritual?

But it's *definitely* a way to bring Chou back.

And other magical girls in the future—though I *pray* it will only be this once.

I put the magazine back in my bag, got up, and opened the door to the stairwell, bumping into Wakana and Tomoko.

Why does it seem like they use the roof as much as I do?

"Sorry about that..."

Wakana flipped her hair in slow motion—combing her fingers through it, gradually lifting and then lowering it. "It's fine."

I walked down to the first landing.

"We saw you with Chou." Tomoko paused. "The last day she was seen."

I stopped in my tracks, making sure I kept a neutral expression when I turned to face them, though my shoulders definitely stiffened when Tomoko spoke. "Oh?"

"You two were standing by a bush, outside the school gates. Fujioka and the others passed by...but then we lost sight of you both because we had to go to the infirmary."

"What we want to know," Wakana continued, "is what you two were talking about. And, of course—if you know anything about her disappearance."

Why are they so curious?

If Masuyo's into paranormal conspiracies—could these two be into more *grounded* mysteries?

"Don't you think I would have gone to the police if I knew anything?"

"Unless you're in on it." Wakana glared down at me. "What was your *business* with Okuma Chou?"

My world was spinning, but I had to keep steady.

I gripped the railing and sighed to calm down.

"There was...a cat under the bush."

"A cat?" the two girls repeated, simultaneously.

"Yeah." I blinked and decided that recounting what had happened couldn't be *too* bad...if I withheld certain information from them, of course. "Well, *first* I asked her why she was crawling around outside the school—and she told me that she was a demon cat?"

"And then?" Wakana prompted.

"I asked her if that was why she was crawling around. And *that's* when she told me there was a cat under the bush. It ran off after Fujioka's group left, so Chou chased after it."

The lie came so *easily*.

I suppose that if we *were* just normal girls who weren't in the center of this entire magical girl operation—it would be the truth.

Chou *would* have run after that cat—because she wouldn't have anywhere else to be.

Or maybe the cat wouldn't have run away—because there wouldn't have been a monster to scare it away.

"Did you happen to see which way she ended up going?" Tomoko asked.

"Not really," I replied. "My allergies started acting up and I got disoriented. She probably ran in that direction..." I waved vaguely in the direction opposite the school gate. "But that's not much to go on.

Besides, I would've told the police if I knew more."

"So she told you about her bow, and then went on her way, huh?" Wakana asked.

"Yeah, she..." I paused.

It didn't seem that either of them had realized Wakana just leaked a detail I didn't mention in my story...

So I wouldn't push it.

"Yeah. She just...*ran off* after that cat."

Tomoko nodded, apparently satisfied with my responses. The two girls walked away, closing the door behind them and leaving me in the stairwell.

I continued walking down the stairs, my mind going a mile a minute.

Maybe Chou just told them about her bow, unprompted, like how she told me. Maybe she tells everybody, and that's why she's not popular.

But why would *those* two come to me and ask about her?

Now that I think about it, the two of them wear *purple* bows in their hair—Tomoko's is in her ponytail, and Wakana's *is* placed similarly to Chou's.

And did Tomoko fidget with hers when Wakana mentioned Chou's?

But *Magical Girl Monthly* didn't mention them having any connection to Chou...so why do they care so much?

008

I decided to hold off on asking Manami—the only person with a confirmed, positive connection to Chou—because she was still mourning.

And because I don't want her to blame me for letting her best friend *die* in battle—which is most likely what would happen if it came out that Chou was Animal Mystery.

Probably.

Or she'd cry—a strong possibility, and not mutually exclusive—but I don't really want to be the one who has to comfort a crying person.

So instead, I went to the school's library and found the previous school year's yearbook.

I flicked through and found Class 2-C's page.

There were many familiar faces...some more familiar than others.

I often forget the other fifteen students who take a back seat to the girls' drama.

You know...I should probably casually introduce myself to the guys at some point—unless that would introduce me to some of *their* drama.

Nope.

No thank you.

Magical girl battles already raise my blood pressure more than enough.

Besides—at least in *Heart-Throbbing Season*—Suzu's "normal" friends take a back seat after the first episode. It seems like anyone without powers isn't important to the plot unless they give the main characters a *reason* to get to where they need to be.

Like a free ticket to a theme park.

Were Suzu's friends even in the first season?

Really have to wonder if the writers couldn't think of how to get Suzu in the park by herself and just...*created* them to give her a reason to get from *Point A* to *Point B*.

I sighed and looked back down at the page, cheek resting on my fist.

Yukiko's name was there...but there was a blank square. Guess her transfer was too late in the year to add her picture.

Chou's picture captured all of her bubbliness in one small rectangle—probably the least formal out of all the pictures on the page.

Amazing how she got away with that pose.

I squinted at Wakana and Tomoko's pictures. They still had their bows.

Well, Wakana did for *sure*—it rested on the back of her hair, but high enough to see it over her head.

Tomoko's hair was in her usual, low ponytail—but there was no guarantee that the bow was holding it in place.

Each class had a spread with a collage of pictures—but there was nothing on Class 2-C's that suggested the three of them were friends, or had even *been* friends at any point.

I flipped to the clubs' pages.

Masuyo, Tsubasa, and Miku—along with some other students—posed with some dingy-looking jars in the *surprisingly popular* Paranormal Club.

I found Nana and Hotaru in the pictures for several sports...but there *has* to be a rule against that, right? There's no way they're in *all* of those...

Manami was holding up a dress for the Sewing Club.

And *then,* I realized that my three classmates may have *not* been in any clubs together in their first year—any *official* clubs with an advisor and five members, at least.

Maybe it was just the three of them—after all, I haven't seen any other students religiously wearing bows in their hair.

Or maybe they weren't even friends anymore in their first year.

They could have had a falling out before first year started—leading the two of them to stay together, still caring about their former friend from a distance...but not doing anything to mend their broken friendship.

Chou didn't really *seem* like the type to hold grudges—sure, she didn't get along with *Aki* and company, but her feelings in that regard were warranted.

Maybe she did something to anger Wakana and Tomoko—and they've only recently gotten over it enough to care about her again?

"What're you doing?"

I practically jumped out of my skin, and slammed the yearbook shut.

Manami blinked at the sound. The circles were gone, but artificially—with the help of frozen spoons or a layer of concealer.

The tired look in her eyes remained, along with a sad glisten.

She had been crying—or was about to start.

Oh God, no one comes to the library this time of day...did she come here to *cry?*

I swallowed and gave my best smile, one that wouldn't give any hint of guilt. "Oh. Hi..."

The pink-haired girl turned the book over, looking at the cover. "Ah, our first year." She looked up at me. "Is...is this about..." She swallowed, barely able to get out: *Chou?*

"Yeah," I replied. "It is."

I really wish we knew what happened to Chou—Manami said, sitting down across from me, caressing the cover.

"Oh, yeah. Me too."

"Like, she was *gonna* come to my house the...the day she went missing. So like, I feel like it's *my* fault, almost. Like if...if she hadn't started on her way to...to *my* house..."

Manami was on the verge of a break down, when the keeper of the *obvious* truth sat before her.

Chou had failed her first attempt at being a magical girl—or at least, *I* had failed for the first time at being the Mascot.

No.

First time implies it'll happen again—and I absolutely *refuse* to allow anyone else to be taken away.

But I can't tell Manami either of these possible truths.

How can I, when I pinky-promised that she wouldn't die—completely confident in myself to answer that she *couldn't*—only now having proof that it's *entirely possible* to die in a battle?

No, I could only watch as Manami opened the yearbook and flipped to the year-old picture of Chou.

And her dam broke.

"Chou…"

I gripped Manami's hand. "She'll come back. They're still searching for her, right? They'll find her! She'll come back."

I wasn't just telling *her* this—I needed to reassure myself, too.

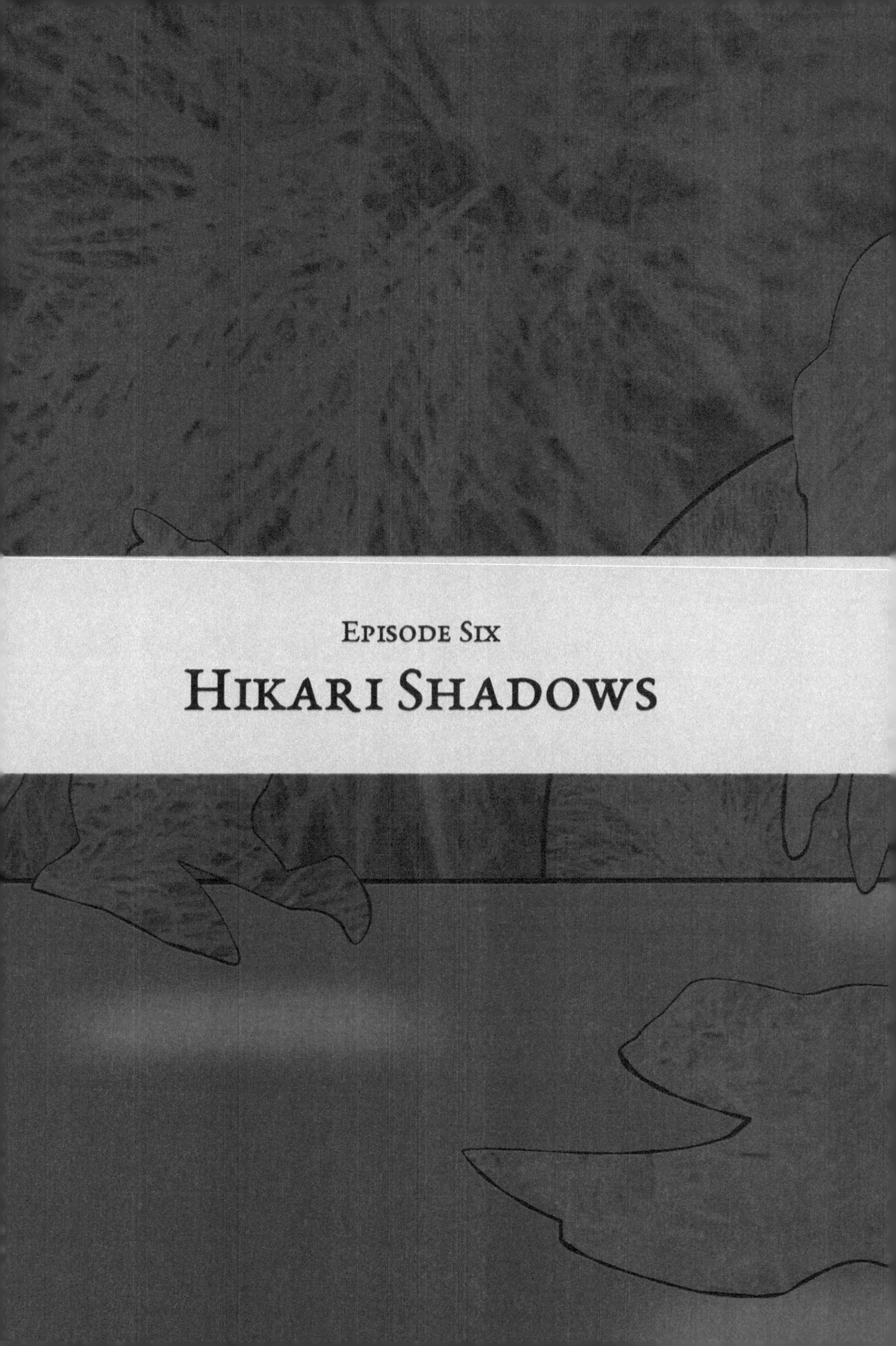

Episode Six

Hikari Shadows

OOI

May twenty-sixth. Today itself has been pretty uneventful, but of course—tomorrow will mark a week since Chou's disappearance.

The *slam* of hands on my desk brought me out of my melancholic trance.

"Takako!" Masuyo exclaimed. "One of these days you absolutely *must* visit the Paranormal Club!"

I blinked. *Why* though?

"No one has told you about the Seven Mysteries of the school yet, right? It's my duty to inform you!"

"Well, I already know that the magical girls showing up are the Seventh Mystery. Can't you just tell me now? Why do I have to go to your clubroom?"

"Sure, I can *tell* you—but you would be missing out on the full *experience*. So, please promise me, Takako—if I tell you about the remaining six, you will visit my clubroom. Yes?"

"All right." I relented.

Masuyo clapped their hands together before pulling up a chair and sitting next to me.

A bit too close.

"Okay! Mystery Number One! In the student council room, there is a portrait of Fujioka Aki!"

"Okay?" Wow, a portrait. And one of Fujioka, no less. Very spooky.

"Outside of school hours, it emits a perfume—something floral, but no one can put their finger on the actual scent."

I wouldn't put it past Fujioka to go in there and spray it with something every day before she leaves to mark her territory. Maybe the scent's from the same artist as *La Puanteur* and that's why no one can place it...

"I know—that one's not really interesting." They shrugged. "That's why it's just the First Mystery. As the number goes up, they get more mysterious."

"...which is why the magical girls are the Seventh Mystery."

"Exactly!" Masuyo adjusted the braid over their shoulder, then tilted their head to the side. "We actually *had* seven already—but the magical girls were too fascinating to ignore! So, I made an *executive decision* to remove the *original* First Mystery and bump everything down by one."

They took out their notebook and laid it open on my desk.

Doodles of wireless signals and phones were crossed out, along with what looked to be the words *The Dead Zone*. The number *one* was also crossed out, with a tiny *zero* scribbled in next to it.

Masuyo turned the page and showed me a framed doodle of Aki. This page was labeled as *The Painting*. The number *two* had the same treatment—crossed out and replaced by a smaller number *one*.

"Nice drawings."

"Thank you!"

Another page turn revealed...tiles?

"Mystery Number Two—The Pipe! It is supposedly within the walls of the girls' toilets, traversing all four floors of the school. When the conditions are right, you can hear conversations from other floors!"

Supposedly? "Have you ever heard it in action?"

"Not personally—but let it be a warning to you to watch what you talk about when washing your hands."

The next page was a drawing of a door.

"Now, this one I *have* witnessed. Mystery Number Three—The Door! The supply closet in the art room has been known to lock itself on occasion when there are occupants. However, it's very consistent. The closet door will only lock when there are two people inside—no more, no less."

"And let me guess—you went in there with another member of the Paranormal Club and got locked in?"

"What? No! How could I *observe* if I were a *participant?* The Art Club gave me a demonstration one day. They showed me that the door doesn't lock from the inside, and two of them stepped inside. Once the door shut, they couldn't get out until someone unlocked it."

Sounds like they were just pranking you, but okay.

"Now, Mystery Number Four is where things get interesting—*The Haunted Locker!*"

"The school is haunted?" I swallowed, thinking of Chou.

"Of *course* not, Takako! Just this locker!" Masuyo tapped the next page, showing a shoe locker. "There's a locker where things go missing, and things are found. For example, if you put an eraser in it before school, at the end of the day it will be gone—sometimes with something to replace it!"

"So, which one is it?" I took note that there was nothing written on the locker's label in the drawing.

"Oh, I haven't found it yet. For some reason, it changes every school year, and there doesn't seem to be a pattern."

"Doesn't that mean it's the entire *entryway* that's haunted?"

Masuyo shook their head. "It's only ever one locker per year."

The next page had a looming shadow.

Humanoid.

"Mystery Number Five—when the sun is directly over the school, a long shadow appears on the roof. With no source."

"A shadow...can't just *not* have a source, right?"

I only got a shrug in response before they moved on.

"And now we are at Mystery Number Six—formerly the most interesting of the seven, usurped by the magical girls—*The Basement.*"

The drawing that Masuyo showed me was of a set of stairs, spiraling downwards.

"But...the school doesn't have a basement." I tilted my head. "Right?"

"This is not a basement that you can access by normal means,

Takako. There's no button for it in either elevator. If you enter the school and go to either stairwell on the first floor—there are no stairs that go down to a sub-level. In fact, public sources say this school is built on a slab of concrete!"

"Then how is there a rumor about a *basement?*"

"If you walk up and down the stairs in a certain pattern, you are supposedly able to come across the basement."

"So...is it door?" And *supposedly?*

"A door, another set of stairs...the accounts vary. Staircases are a liminal space. Students tend to find the basement accidentally, so the pattern is not known. It is *difficult* to keep track of where you have been in the school if you are wandering aimlessly, yes?"

"I guess..."

Masuyo closed their notebook and pocketed it. "Well, my apologies for keeping you. I am aware you wander the school during your free time, but it seemed this would be the best time to talk, yes?"

"Yeah, I guess. Thanks for the info. It was...interesting."

They beamed at me.

OO2

I hummed as I flipped through *Magical Girl Monthly.*

Once again, I was lounging on the roof in the shade of the stairwell.

Thankfully, I have yet to be up here during the precise window to witness the Fifth Mystery.

Running my fingers along the edge of the magazine, I realized that there were no gaps—the strips that I had torn out had regenerated, leaving the side of the issue smooth, flat, and pristine.

It was like new.

Mint condition.

An *Eighth* Mystery, maybe?

Guess that answers Manami's question—it won't matter if anyone loses their paper, since I'm apparently able to make infinite transformation trinkets.

Unless the pages only regenerated because everyone lost track of their papers?

In which case—wow, no one was able to keep them safe for very long.

As soon as that thought surfaced, I bit my tongue in regret, once again thinking of Chou.

Did her transformation paper regenerate immediately at the end of that battle?

I can't remember.

Lunch is almost over, so I'll have to go back to class soon—and figure out how to get *Hikari* alone long enough to transform her for the battle.

Judging by the information available in the magazine, the monsters this time around—Shadows—seem like they'll be *stronger* than usual...

But *why* will they be stronger?

Yes, shadows are dark, and there's a primal *fear* of them when you're a kid...but they're created by the presence of *light,* and so they don't have a physical form—they can't *hurt* you, they can't *touch* you...

Well, actually, they *can* touch you—but you usually don't give it much thought, so it's not something you'd notice.

I placed the magazine down and held out my left hand. Slowly, I raised my other hand, casting a shadow on my left palm.

I *guess* if I did this for a while, the shaded area would feel cooler than the rest of me, out here in the sun.

If I were sitting under a tree, I'd definitely feel cooler than I am now—sitting directly *in* the sun.

Regardless, I just don't get it.

Shadows don't have a form, so why should there be any fear of them? If I saw a large shadow, I'd be more afraid of what's *creating* it.

Its source.

Maybe *that's* the fear's origin.

So—what's creating *these* monstrous Shadows?

Could the Shadows be related somehow to the Fifth Mystery?

Could they have appeared on the roof before?

I picked up the magazine and flipped to the section with monsters once again, and an additional line caught my eye: *Let him out.*

I blinked.

Who exactly am I supposed to be letting out?

OO3

Cleaning duty—the rare occasion that Hikari is away from Aki and her fellow lackeys.

I picked up a wet rag and joined her in cleaning the blackboard. "Hey."

She glanced at me, briefly. "Hello."

"So..."

Hikari continued wiping, tuning out my sentence filler.

What should I even talk to her about?

What topic will immediately pull her in?

"So I heard your mother is a CEO? What company?"

"The Nakajima Conglomerate."

"Oh. What..." I paused to focus my attention on a buildup of chalk—someone's poor attempt at drawing an *aiai-gasa.* "What does she do there?"

"What she does is *far* beyond your ken. You wouldn't understand even if I gave you the *simple* explanation."

Wow, okay.

I dunked the rag and went back to the lighter chalk dust.

Wait a minute.

Didn't someone tell me that Hikari never specified what company her mother owned?

I mean, sure—looking at it now, it's kinda *obvious* that *Nakajima* Hikari's mother would be the CEO of the *Nakajima* Conglomerate—but *still!*

I might be on the verge of a breakthrough with her!

"*So!*" I squeezed the rag against the board in glee, watching the water trickle down. "What do *you* like to do for *fun?*"

"Are you *seriously* trying to play a game with me to pass the time as we clean?" she asked, dunking the rag and going in for another swipe.

"Maybe. What's so wrong with that?"

"I understand that you missed the first two weeks of school—either on purpose or not—but you *must* understand that's when key friendships are formed in school. You *had* your chance to befriend me at the same time Fujioka extended her hand to you. Instead, you chose to side with the *undesirables* of our class."

"Undesirables? Seems like they're more popular than your lot."

Nicer, too—I muttered.

"You clearly haven't interacted with the rest of the student body—Aki is the most popular girl in school!"

"Whatever—we'll still have to get along sooner or later, though. Right? For the cultural festival and stuff?"

"Yes. But that will be a temporary extension of the olive branch, where we come together in a team building exercise and make something out of a combined effort. The truth is that—in the grand scheme of things—it won't be anything but a conversation topic for reunions."

Again, *wow.* "So in that case—is your friendship with Fujioka a temporary truce?"

Hikari paused mid-swipe. "What do you mean by *that?*" she retorted.

The year was intact, but today's date was a wet smear.

"What do you see in Fujioka? I mean, she's kinda stuck up. She acts like she's so *important,* like a princess—but she hurts others' feelings. If she had it in her, I have no doubt she'd probably cause *more* than just psychological damage." I dipped the rag in the bucket. "She's a *bully*—but you always defend her when she's called out on it. You seem to know she's bad—so why would you hang out with her unless there was some sort of benefit? Especially when it seems like you look at everything from the perspective of what you can potentially gain. What could you *possibly* gain—aside from not being one of the classmates she bullies?"

Hikari stared at me with wide eyes before looking around, making sure no one was loitering in the classroom. She closed her eyes and let out a harrowing sigh. "You didn't *know* her...back when *I* met her."

Huh. "Was she any different than she is now?"

The white-haired girl blinked, turning back to the board. "Not at all," she said, quickly, obviously caught in a lie.

"So, she *was* different..."

"She *wasn't* different," Hikari huffed, squeezing the rag against the board, "but she also wasn't the same... I will confess, I suppose I'm *partly* to blame—for fueling her narcissism all these years—but something about being next to her has always felt so amazing. I *suppose* that's the *benefit* that you mentioned."

How could Fujioka have been different and the same all at once?

Hikari concentrated on wiping hypnotizing wet circles, muttering to herself, *The two of us were happy, then the three of us, and then the two of us...*

I tilted my head. "Three of you?"

This brought Hikari out of her trance. "What?"

Darn. I should've let her continue talking to herself.

"You just said that two of you were happy, then three, then back to two. Who was the third?" I squeezed my rag. It was a pure hunch, but I had to ask, *Was it Chou?*

Hikari laughed, a couple snorts thrown in. "*What?*" she screeched between gasps. She coughed on chalk dust. "*Okuma?* No, she's like a kid that needs babysitting! Or—*needed,* excuse me."

So Aki and company weren't mean to Chou because she used to be in their clique—not really any surprise there—but who was the *third* friend, then?

Manami?

Probably.

"Anyway—why am I even *entertaining* you?" Hikari asked. She dropped her rag into the bucket, then shook her hands dry before resting them on her hips. "I finished *my* side of the board, so pick up the slack. If this was your *job,* I'd fire you on the spot and have you blacklisted." She turned, her pigtails bouncing, and walked out of the classroom—probably to look for Aki.

Well...at least I broke the ice before having to recruit her to fight some sentient Shadows, right?

OO4

The paths in the Darkness weren't linear—they kept moving, ever changing.

Kenji walked alone, his battle axe slung over his shoulder like a stick without a polka-dotted bindle.

He walked in a straight line, making no turns—and yet he still passed through his usual play area at *least* five times, each from a different direction.

The first time Kenji saw his toys from a new angle, he got excited, thinking it was a new place for him to play. He even sat down with them before realizing they were the same old, broken toys.

The next few times, he didn't pause, continuing down his straight path, shifting his axe to drag it behind him.

He refused to stop.

"I wanna *leave* this stupid place!" Kenji tossed his axe to the ground. "You're all being *mean* to me!"

Once more, he had come across his play area. He scrunched up his nose then took a running start, kicking a one-eyed plushie out of a pile.

Its stuffing flew out, scattering everywhere.

"Gahh!" Kenji ran to fetch his axe and *zoomed* back to the plushie, swinging it above his head to—

"And *what* would you be willing to *give up?*"

Kenji stumbled over his own feet as he screeched to a halt and looked around, the axe falling to the ground behind him with a *clang*.

It was his father's voice—*that* he was sure of...but his usual presence was missing.

His father may have been in the Darkness, but he was nowhere nearby.

Kenji hesitantly reached for the plushie and scooped it up in both hands.

The closest animal it could be described as was a *bear*—but even *that* was a stretch.

He squeezed its stomach and small pieces of stuffing fell from its empty socket.

Its single glass eye stared back at him—a glint of light with no source silently pleaded that he stop.

You need to keep part of the Darkness with you, or else you can never return—it was his father's voice again.

There was no way he was imagining this, and it wasn't some sort of dream.

The voice was definitely coming from the bear.

The stuffing gradually tumbled out of the gaping hole, but it was building in momentum.

There was far more stuffing than it was possible for the bear to hold—and this stuffing turned viscous, oozing out and coating Kenji's hand.

"You're *weak,* Kenji. Too *weak.*"

"No, I'm not!" the boy shrieked, either at the bear or his father— highly likely it was targeted at both. He throttled the bear. "Let me *out!*"

The stuffing was red, and any contact it made with his skin was warm but cold, wet but dry.

What happened next burned for a moment...

005

Leaving the blackboard unfinished, I grabbed my bag from my desk and walked out of the classroom after Hikari, looking both ways to see which way she went.

The fluorescents at the end of the hall to my right flickered before dying.

One right after the other.

The lights shut off with a loud *hum*.

Huumm.

Huumm.

Huumm.

Then again, that could've just been my pulse quickening in my ears.

Hikari walked in the opposite direction, so this strange occurrence went unnoticed on her part.

I took a few quick steps to catch up. "Hey, Hikari…"

Without turning around: *That's Nakajima to you.*

"Okay—*Nakajima*. I…" I looked over my shoulder at the approaching darkness. "There's something I need to show you."

Hikari didn't stop walking. In fact, she may have sped up a bit to get to her destination faster.

I stumbled to keep up.

"Elevator pitch, please."

"Ele—*huh?*"

"You need to *persuade me* in *one sentence* to listen to the rest of what you have to say." Hikari spun around on her heel to face me. "Why you would even *try* talking to me without *any idea* of what an elevator pitch is—it's beyond me. I'm *far* too busy for—" Something behind me caught her attention. "Wait...do you *see* that?"

"See what?" I asked, feigning ignorance.

"It's my interest in continuing this conversation with you. It just left, probably to clean up the rest of the blackboard—because I *know* that there's no way you could have done a satisfactory job of it. Now, if you'll *excuse* me, I have an important appointment to attend to."

Hikari turned and continued walking down the hall.

Well *that* didn't work. But I *have* to intercept her before she gets to Fujioka and the others—because how am I going to explain why I need to get her alone?

The Shadows that were quickly gaining on us continued to go unnoticed by her—sliding and swirling around the walls, floor, and ceiling as though they were a layer of paint being applied haphazardly.

I looked to my left and right where the hallways intersected—the Shadows came from both directions there, too—I couldn't make out anything.

"Nakajima, please wait!" I ran after her, catching the stairwell's door.

Hikari started walking up, not taking notice of the Shadows descending from the fourth floor.

Not only were they coating every surface in the stairwell, but they were now expanding and spreading through the air, making it thicker like a starless night sky.

She turned to face me. "Leave me *alone,* Kurosawa."

"I need you to become a magical girl. *Right. Now.* How's *that* for an elevator pitch?"

"A *what?*" Hikari raised an eyebrow. "I have *no* time to play *make-believe* with you. I'm not your *babysitter.*"

I let the door close and gestured up the stairs as I walked towards her. "Are you *really* not noticing the *Shadows* closing in?"

"You're scared of the *dark,* too?"

I have no idea what will happen if I go without transforming and lending power to a magical girl—*especially* with an enemy that seems as simple as the Shadows.

Is there something hiding in the Shadows?

Will I be grabbed and swallowed whole...like how the Vines took Chou?

Or will everything be fine?

I don't have time for this, Hikari muttered—turning back around to face an impassible wall of darkness on the step above her. "What—"

"Do you believe me now?"

"Of course not. You were *obviously* distracting me so someone could...could place...a large wooden *board* behind me." She crossed her arms. "I have to say, though—it *is* impressive. I didn't know it was possible to paint something to look *this* dark. *And* there are no paint strokes showing. It looks like a void."

Taking her by the wrist, I pulled her off the bottom step before she could reach out to touch the darkness.

"Let go of me!" Hikari shouted as she stumbled and smacked my hand away from her. "Don't *touch* me!"

The Shadows advanced—were they angered by the sudden loud noise?

The lights outside of the stairwell were off—only the door shielded us from the darkness out there.

"Are you *really* not seeing any of this?" I asked, gesticulating at it.

"It's a power outage, Kurosawa. Of *course* I can't." Hikari stood there with her arms crossed, unamused.

"Didn't you notice the *way* that the lights were turning off? That we're currently under the *only* light that hasn't gone out?"

"*Obviously,* Kurosawa. And as I *told* you, I have a prior engagement that I was trying to get to. I had no time for formalities, and now I'm unable to safely traverse the stairs because the *you-shaped* wrench in the works didn't let me reach them in time." She sighed and reached into her pocket, taking out her phone—presumably to use the flashlight.

I really don't want us to transform where anyone can see from within the darkness, but I guess we have no choice...

"Here!" I pulled out my copy of *Magical Girl Monthly,* flipped to the correct page, and tore out Hikari's paper strip.

It was pale yellow with white diamonds and sparkles. Even though the design wasn't printed on holographic paper and didn't include actual glitter, the paper seemed like it was emitting or reflecting light.

"Just take this!"

"Don't just hand me your garbage!" Hikari tried throwing it away, but the paper stuck to her fingers like plastic with static cling.

I knelt down, my tongue twisting through the usual speech at a speed that Nana would be proud of.

The Shadows cut off the stairs completely now, and not even the light produced by Hikari's transformation could dispel it.

Hikari's phone clattered to the floor—screen facing up, thankfully—as the strip of paper slithered up her arm, wrapping around her neck to become a choker. A translucent yellow scarf emerged from her throat, looping around to the back and connecting to itself. A light yellow, sleeveless pleated tailcoat over a black romper replaced her school uniform. The drop tail emitted rainbow lights. Yellow stilettos gave her a boost in height. Her scrunchies remained in her pigtails, though they seemed to be a paler yellow—no longer the garish shade assigned by the school.

"What..." Hikari looked down at herself. "What just happened?"

She turned to my body, still in its kneeling position.

"Kurosawa, I *asked* you, what did you *do?*"

Hikari finally noticed the Shadows as they closed in—

But she *didn't* notice the open portal until she took a step backwards, falling right through it.

oo6

"Where are we?"

"Hm."

That's really a good question.

Up until now, each species of monster had its own domain...but this seems to be a repeat of the Suits' world.

"Kurosawa? I *asked* you a *question!*"

"The Black World—"

"Oh, how *original.* We're in complete *darkness* and you decide to go with the first name that comes to mind—"

Of course, it's a working title, I replied—giving my best impression of someone who was wise beyond their years.

Hikari rolled her eyes. "Kurosawa, I have a *very* important meeting I must attend. Just let me *go,* and I will make sure to leave this out of your annual performance review."

"We—" I scowled. "Nakajima, why would you need to write a performance review for me? We're *students.* I'm your *classmate.* I don't *work* for you—*no one* here *works* for you!"

"Not *yet.*"

"Agh!" I stamped my foot, and the metal clang reverberated through this dimension. "You're such a *pain!* I'm supposed to be a *happy* magical girl *mascot!*" I tried to put as many tired, sarcastic sparkles as I could into my voice. "But *you!*" I stepped forward, getting in her face. "*You* are just the last straw, Miss *Business!*" I flicked her forehead.

She pushed my hand away with her wrist—again, what are the rules of my tangibility in these worlds?—and tried glaring back at me.

Of course, her focus was off a little bit since she couldn't see me.

"*Seriously,* Nakajima. You're going through life acting like everyone's going to be *below* you when you strike it rich—but what happens if someone you treated horribly becomes more successful than you?"

"I don't need to hear this from *you* right now, Kurosawa. Where's the exit?" Hikari looked off to the side before turning back to me. "I *want* to *leave!*"

With her outburst, Shadows unpeeled from the floor around us and started dancing about.

La la- la, la la- la!

They had multiple appendages, but it seemed like they couldn't decide what they were supposed to be—one moment the lumps took turns acting as limbs, wobbling and shuffling and cartwheeling, but the next, one would seem to take the lead as its head, staying upright and shifting around as though looking at us.

"What are *those?*"

I looked at the ground where they came from and realized that they left behind gray silhouettes.

So this is really the *Gray* World.

"You have to fight them."

"Kurosawa, I may be *dressed* as a magical girl—how you pulled that off is still beyond me—but I am *not* a magical girl, and I *refuse.*"

Okay.

Speech time.

"You think that being a magical girl is below you, so just like any other responsibility that you think you're too good for, you push it away."

"Well, it *is* below me. Magical girls are a *childish* genre, and I'm on my way to becoming a successful *adult* in the business world. *Besides*—I can't put *this* on my résumé! I'd make a total fool out of myself!"

"Nakajima, you're *sixteen*. There's plenty of time to build the résumé that you want."

The Shadows danced closer, making garbled noises that sounded like *Wanna go! Wanna leave!*

"No, there's *not!* There's so much that has to be done to prepare!" She held herself and shook as she backed away from me. There was nowhere she could escape to with the monsters approaching—making the only option to collapse in on herself.

Let me go! Let me go! Wanna go! Wanna leave!

"You've already done so much to prepare, just slow down."

No!

Hikari screamed—and a radial rainbow blast emerged from her chest, taking out the incoming Shadows. I had to cover my eyes to avoid being blinded.

"I have to prove myself! *Everything* I do she compares to something she's done and asks why I haven't accomplished more. I'll bring home a paycheck—she'll say that by my age hers was *double*." She looked up at me. "That's why I don't have time for this, Takako. I need to focus on the *future*. I need to prove myself to her and step out of her shadow."

It doesn't seem like she's talking about Aki...

So could it be...

"Hikari, you're *already* out of your mother's shadow." I placed my hand on her shoulder. "Maybe you were never even in it to begin with."

"Huh?" A look of confusion—but less *What are you talking about?* and more like I hit the nail on the head, *How did you psychoanalyze me, new kid?*

"You're Light Mystery. You have the power to dispel any shadow with a brightness that no one else possesses."

"Figuratively, you mean?"

"No." I pulled away and gestured at her. "Look at yourself—you're *glowing*. You have the power to light your own way. You're emitting your *own* light, dispelling any shadow that you think you may be in. *You* get to decide how you live your own life—there's no need to compare yourself to her anymore."

"In that case, if I get to decide..." Hikari straightened her back. "If *I* get to decide, I suppose I *should* give this a try. We're here after all, so I might as well."

I gave her a thumbs up and smiled. "That's the spirit!"

Can't believe that worked...

"What's my first move?"

"Hold your right hand out—like you're holding a *flashlight* or a *pen*." I walked around Hikari, tapping a hand on her back and placing the other on her forearm to fix her form.

"Which is it? Kurosawa, those two things have completely different grips. I'm assuming you're teaching me to summon a weapon—I don't want to stab myself if I'm holding it wrong."

"Could be some other third thing. Maybe lipstick?"

"*'Maybe'?*" Hikari shifted her hand and a crystalline cylinder—no, it was a triangular prism—appeared from nowhere, its end chiseled like lipstick and cycling through myriad colors.

A rainbow stretched out, but it was limp like a ribbon or a whip. It pooled at the ground, tangling around itself like a toddler's first attempt at tying their shoes...

Or was it becoming a blob, like the result of that same toddler stepping on a tube of toothpaste?

Wherever it touched the ground, the black Shadows dispersed and revealed the gray backdrop of their world.

"Whip your arm, Hikari!"

"O-Okay!" She extended her arm above her head, and the mass of rainbow glop followed, smacking her in the face. "Gah!" Hikari took two steps back, elbowing me in the gut as she rubbed her nose.

The crystal shattered into a cloud of glitter in her hand.

A few Shadows rose up in the distance and slowly approached...with caution?

Second-hand embarrassment?

"Is this how your other magical girl colleagues performed for their first battles?" she asked, lowering her hand from her face as she turned to me.

The bridge of her nose was pink—though that coloration was already starting to fade—and her eyes were watering.

"It's really a grab bag of skill levels." I held up her elbow in the correct position again. "I'll be the first to admit that was my fault, though. I should've told you to whip it sooner—before it all pooled at your feet."

Hikari's mouth flattened, but she summoned the crystal again.

This time, she didn't wait for instruction and immediately brought her arm up.

The premature rainbow tangled around her arm and head, wrapping around the rest of her body.

Hikari released the crystal, letting it shatter in midair.

She glared at me accusingly.

"You're not going to be the best at everything the first time you try it, you know."

"Oh, I'm *well* aware."

Well, third time's the charm, *right?*

Hikari held her arm out once more, summoning the crystal and the rainbow. She didn't raise her arm as quickly as the previous attempt, and didn't wait as long as when I first instructed her.

The rainbow flicked out and hit one of the Shadows, twisting around one of its currently designated legs and causing it to stumble a bit.

Hikari gave me a bright, magical girl smile and fist-pumped. "Yes! I did it!"

However, even though it stumbled—the Shadow still continued to press forward, turning that leg into its head.

"No!" she grunted, yanking the whip back with both hands.

The Shadow *puff*ed into a small cloud of dust.

Hikari let out an exasperated sigh.

"Being a magical girl is difficult work," I said. "Like any job, there's a learning curve."

"Well, are there any *other* attacks I can use? This rainbow whip is *clearly* not working for me."

007

I stood before a seemingly endless black wall—the threshold that led to the largest Shadow. I placed my gloved hand flat on it and got a gelatinous ripple in response.

"Are you ready?"

"Of course not," Hikari replied, forming the prism in her hand in preparation for the battle and whipping the rainbow off to the side to make a show of it.

Effortlessly, the rainbow hit the last tiny Shadow.

"That was pure luck," she insisted. "I have absolutely no confidence that I'll be able to defeat the giant Shadow."

"Well, can you muster some up?"

"Kurosawa—you've seen my incompetency."

Well, I wouldn't say *that*—

"I have low expectations for how the following battle will go—and for once, they aren't based off of *someone else's* preconceived notions of me. They're based on solid evidence: I am a magical blunder."

Where's she going with this?

"And do you know what? I'm all right with that. I've made my peace with what I'm capable of as a magical girl. All that matters is that I'm trying out a new *experience*. That's how those hero shows for children go, right? Some kids I've babysat had something like that playing on the television."

Down, but not out—she continued. "Fall down seven times—get up eight."

Not going to say anything to jinx it...

"Let's go. Like I said, I'm not ready for this, and probably never will be—but it's better that I try than to never take the final step."

And with that—we took that final step, into the darkness.

Let me go!

Hot musty air pushed past us—*through* us—as though the darkness itself exhaled.

Hikari held up a hand, palm up, summoning a small orb of light to look around.

"I don't see the monster," she murmured.

I followed her, closely. "Stay on your toes—it could be anywhere."

Between Hikari's heels tapping and my armored boots clanging was a steady breath.

Tap. Tap. Clang. Clang.

Exhale.

Tap. Tap. Clang. Clang.

Inhale.

"It feels like we're not getting anywhere..." Hikari stopped walking. "Kurosawa, shouldn't we be reaching the monster soon?"

I stopped and looked at Hikari. Her light didn't dance like a flame, and instead acted more like a lightbulb the way it illuminated the concern on her face.

I pivoted and looked back to where we had come from—there was only darkness behind us.

Darkness everywhere.

No walls or exit in sight.

I turned back to Hikari—but she wasn't there.

Instead, I saw myself.

No, a *reflection* of myself—in the pure black pupil of a giant eyeball.

White with a green iris, the lidless eye hovered in front of me.

Wanna leave!

"Then leave," I replied.

Let me go!

I'm not keeping you here—I muttered, taking a step away from the eye. It didn't follow like I expected, and kept hovering in that stationary position.

Unblinking, thankfully.

What would a blink from it even *look* like?

"H-Hikari?" I called out. "Where are you?"

No response.

At least I know she's not *gone* gone, like Chou—that scythe hasn't appeared in my hands.

Yet.

Giving one last look at the eyeball, I turned in the direction I assumed that I had come from, tucked my head down—and ran.

Probably not the best idea to run without watching *where* I was running *to*—because I tripped over something and fell to the ground.

I rolled over to look.

It was a dark form.

"Hikari?" I asked, stretching out my foot to give it a light tap.

Ngh, the form replied.

"Hikari...that's you, right?" I sat up and scooted over to it. "Hikari?"

Lemme go...

"Okay—*not* Hikari. Got it."

I let out a quiet groan as I stood and continued on my search for Hikari, the final Shadow, and the exit.

Then, out of nowhere—a blast of light.

"Hikari?"

She stood silhouetted against a circular opening that had been created by the blinding light.

"Kurosawa!" Hikari whipped the rainbow towards me. "Grab it!"

I cowered away from it.

Sure, it's just a sharp smack for *her* that leaves behind some stinging, red skin—but it turns Shadows to *dust*. Who knows what'll happen if I'm on its receiving end? And regardless, I don't want to get smacked by a rainbow whip, thank you very much.

The whip *smack*ed the ground—which turned gray.

"Huh?"

The rainbow started to slowly retract like a measuring tape.

I turned to look for the lumpy form on the ground that I had tripped over—maybe I could see who it really was with the light from the opening Hikari had made.

However, there was no such shape.

Not even the floating eyeball!

"Kurosawa, come on! The opening's closing!"

Sure enough, it was—Hikari looked like something out of an anime—the final scene, ending with an iris shot.

I raced to her—neck and neck with the rainbow—and dove through the shrinking opening, landing on the gray floor.

Looking over my shoulder, I saw the opening had disappeared—it was back to being a black wall.

"What the—"

"*Genius* move, Kurosawa. Absolutely *brilliant*. And to think *you're* supposed to be *my* mentor."

I stood and put my hands on my hips. "Hikari—what's going on?"

To answer me, she summoned her rainbow and whipped at the black wall between words. "This! Is! The! Largest! Shadow!"

Ashy scars appeared on the wall's surface, but they quickly healed as soon as Hikari's attack ceased.

"Oh my God..." I furrowed my brow. "Wait...how did *you* get out?"

"The same way *you* just did—I made an exit with my powers."

"But you were just ahead of me, and I turned around to see where we had come from! When I turned back, you had disappeared—so how did you end up *here?*"

Hikari shrugged.

"And...you didn't happen to *see* anything in there, did you?"

"No. What are you even talking about? It was just dark in there."

Should I have saved that speech about being *blinded by hatred* for *you,* Hikari?

Should I repeat myself?

I settled for muttering, *Don't worry about it.*

Hikari created an orb of light in her palms and pressed it against the wall. There was some resistance—before it forced its way through, pulling the Shadow behind it like rippling fabric.

234

She sidestepped to the right, created another orb, and shoved it into the wall once more.

Hikari continued doing this while I just stood by and watched.

The holes Hikari punctured into the wall allowed us to get a glimpse of the Gray World beyond it. Judging by how far we had walked into the darkness, we should have been able to reach the other side of the wall.

But something was off—I had perceived the darkness as being an endless expanse, while Hikari only acknowledged this as a mild annoyance, able to exit at any time.

Speaking of which…

With all these holes cut into the Shadow like Swiss cheese, letting in the ambient light of the Gray World—I couldn't see the eyeball or the form I had tripped over, when I clearly should have.

Wait a minute.

For all previous battles, the Final Boss—for lack of a better term— was a giant version of the smaller monsters. Except maybe the Vines?

So.

"Hikari," I said. "Don't you think it's weird?"

"What?" she asked, continuing to attack the wall.

"That this Shadow is just a wall. Unmoving. Not attacking us."

"Kurosawa, I have no baseline for how giant monsters work."

Well, that *is* true…

"But now that you mention it, I do suppose it's strange. Though I'm not going to complain—it's an easy target, so we'll be able to leave sooner than expected."

That's also true.

A bit curious, I started walking away from the Shadow.

"Where are you going?" Hikari asked.

"Don't worry," I replied over my shoulder. "You just keep doing what you're doing."

Once I was far enough away, I looked at the massive Shadow.

At this distance, it was easier to see what we had missed—it wasn't an endless wall.

Instead, it had an irregular form like the smaller Shadows.

A round knoll at the center, with a longer, tapered form on the right, and a smaller mound on the left.

I squinted at that smaller mound—it had its own cluster of lumps protruding from it.

And it was when I squinted—that it shifted.

The eyeball drilled its way out of the gelatinous Shadow's bubbling blackness. It spiraled around before its gaze straightened—focusing on Hikari, who was still attacking it.

The final piece of the puzzle.

This Shadow *wasn't* a generic lump of lumps on lumps—but a toy bear.

A *giant* toy bear, lying on its back, presumably discarded by a child proportional to it.

The Shadow's arm slid against the floor towards her, slowly at first, then gaining speed.

"Hikari! Watch out!"

"Huh?"

I expected the arm to launch Hikari through the air in my direction. I expected the scythe to appear in my hands again.

However, she was absorbed once more, the way we had entered the Shadow earlier—and since it was a moving arm and not the immobile torso, she was subsequently ejected out the other side.

Visibly shaken.

"I *said* to watch out!" I called out as I ran back to her. It seemed the distance I had to traverse to get back to the Shadow was halved, like being in a dream.

As I reached her side, I expected her to say something like, *And you distracted me, so how could I watch out?*

Instead, she threw herself at me and sobbed into my shoulder.

Uh...

What?

Sniffle.

I patted her on the back and looked straight ahead—into the Shadow's arm that was coming back towards us.

"Hikari—brace yourself."

I hugged her tightly on the off chance we might get separated.

Without moving from where we stood, we entered the Shadow once more—another gelatinous entrance.

"Hikari—"

Sob, sob!

"Hikari, listen—before it's too late, you have to *fight*. While we're still in its arm, hurry! Summon your rainbow...or that other light!"

"I *can't!*"

"Didn't we go over this earlier? You said you'd *try*."

"I *did* try, Kurosawa! You saw me! The small Shadows were no problem. When I thought this was a wall, it was *fine!* But this is *impossible,* and we're going to *die* where we stand."

"No, you're not!"

Somehow, I could feel the Shadow's movement. With little foresight, I shoved Hikari away from me. She landed on the gray floor outside, on her butt, before looking up at me as I was reabsorbed into the Shadow.

"K-Kurosawa?!"

I closed my eyes and hugged myself.

Kurosawa?! What are you thinking?!

From where I stood, she sounded muffled, as though I was underwater.

Kurosawa, please! I can't do this by myself!

I inhaled through my nose.

And exhaled through my mouth.

Takako!

Like how she had destroyed the Shadows that had surrounded us when we first arrived, the radial rainbow blast returned from her chest— her heart—and disintegrated the Shadow's arm.

Leaving me standing there, in one piece.

"Don't you *dare* do that again," Hikari growled. Then, in a possible attempt to brush off her caring about my well-being, she added, "I refuse to be left alone here when I don't even know how to leave."

"Do you think you'll be able to summon that power again on your own?" I asked.

"I don't *know,*" she replied, rubbing her eyes with the backs of her hands. "It's not like I *tried* to do that before. It was an accident!"

"In that case, you may not like my solution for a quick victory."

Hikari lowered her hands. "Kurosawa, you had *better not* attempt what I think you're going to. Don't you *dare* leave me to pick up the pieces after you fulfill some self-sacrificial dream of yours."

"My dreams aren't filled with *self-sacrifice*—they're filled with a faceless, flan-loving princess."

"That sounds *terrifying*."

"Hey—*don't* insult Flan Girl." I pointed at her.

She hiccuped back a confused sob.

"Look. That big attack seems to be the only thing that does real damage to this Shadow. So either you muster up the courage to use that attack—or I have to go back inside the Shadow and *scare* it out of you."

Hic!

"Along with those hiccups." I summoned my spoon and some vanilla pudding. "It's your choice."

Hikari closed her eyes and scowled, before extending her arms out to the sides in an attempt to summon the much-needed rainbow attack.

After a moment, she opened her eyes—and looked disappointed when the Shadow was still there.

"I suppose we'll have to go with that second option." Hikari then added through a sigh, *No matter how much I hate it.*

"That's the spirit!"

She gave me a dirty look.

oo8

Hikari's face was still a little puffy from crying, but the way she held herself was much lighter. The giant Shadow was gone, but we both knew what overshadows her in our world isn't as easy to defeat.

"Hey," I said, holding out a gloved hand. "If you ever want to talk..."

Hikari gave a cursory glance to my beckoning hand before flicking her eyes up to meet mine.

Without a word, she walked through the portal.

I closed my eyes.

One moment, I was in the Gray World—and the next I was sitting in the school stairwell, now fully lit, save for a slight flicker of the fluorescents.

Hikari gazed down at me with her arms crossed. She had a soft look of concern in her eyes that quickly dispersed when she saw me wake.

Of course—as soon as we return to school, she's back to business as usual.

"We're keeping this a secret between the two of us." She turned her head away from me. "Don't start thinking this is the same as a budding friendship."

"Don't worry," I replied. "I didn't expect us to suddenly become friends."

Hikari gave a satisfactory nod. "Good." She stretched her face, wiping one stray tear from the corner of her eye with her pinky.

"That being said…it still feels like a window's been opened." I stood and leaned against the railing. "Maybe we're not friends *now*—but this secret could be what drives us to become closer in the future."

Hikari grimaced.

"Well, maybe just casual acquaintances." I added, hastily, *After all, why would you throw away a potential partnership that could be beneficial?*

"How could being a *magical girl* be beneficial for my future?"

"Networking?"

"I doubt it, Kurosawa—any connections I make when I'm transformed won't count because I'm going by an alternative name."

"You could *probably* find a way to send them in your direction."

She huffed. "And draw attention to a possible connection between *Nakajima Hikari* and *Light Mystery*? No—thank you. I'd rather not be put in danger as someone close to a *person of interest*."

"Hikari, I'm *sure* that there's a way."

"Oh? Do you have any suggestions?"

I hummed and kicked at an imaginary stone.

"Right. I thought so."

"Since you don't want to be friends now, maybe you will when we're older and out of high school—or university, or whatever happens next. Because what happens if I'm more successful than you? You said you didn't need to hear it from me then, but I really want to know. If *I* end up more successful than *you,* are you gonna come crawling to me and ask me to pardon your rudeness?"

"I highly doubt there's any measure of success one can think of that you can one up me in."

Wow. You *really* do *not* think highly of me. "Maybe…happiness?"

"How does one measure *happiness?* Besides, you could look at my life and say 'yes, *I,* Kurosawa Takako, am *much* more happier than Nakajima Hikari!' and declare yourself the victor."

"Hm. I mean, I wouldn't. But I suppose we're at an impasse, in that case."

Though judging by how many stress-tears you cried during your battle, I'm pretty sure I've got a leg up in the competition—even considering my current state of amnesia.

Not that we're *competing,* or *should* compete in something like levels of happiness—that seems really unhealthy and stressful, something I do *not* want to partake in.

The door to the fourth floor opened, and footsteps echoed in the stairwell.

"Hikari~" a voice chimed in from above us.

"Aki!" the white-haired girl beamed, brushing past me as she skipped up a couple stairs.

The blonde came down to the landing, eclipsing the light from the window behind her. Yukiko and Aoi were at her heels. "You were running late for our meeting, so we were going to come find you. But then the power went out, so we had to wait in the council room."

"Thank you for your concern." Hikari laced her fingers behind her. "I suppose it *is* getting late...shall we have our discussion on the way to your house?"

Aki smiled. "Of course! I can't *bear* to stay on campus for longer than necessary." The trio walked down the stairs, meeting Hikari, and then the four of them walked past me.

Yeah, especially with the chance of another blackout, Yukiko agreed.

"Oh?" Aoi tilted her head.

"Well, if there's one power outage, it means that it's more likely there'll be another, right?"

Hikari let out a short laugh. "I don't think that's how blackouts work."

Their conversation faded as they walked down the hall and around the corner.

And I was blissfully forgotten.

I made my way back to the classroom and sighed—*really* not in the mood to continue washing the blackboard, but *whatever.*

A blackboard is a board that's black, until white chalk makes first contact. Therefore, a blackboard is truly pristine only on the day it's installed.

I was expecting to see the board in its sullied state, with chalk scribbles that were partially cleaned.

What I saw instead was a blackboard.

A board that's black—good as new, as though it had never been touched by chalk.

I dropped my bag and stood in front of it, staring at this black wall.

If it were a green chalkboard, or a whiteboard, I probably wouldn't be this hypnotized.

This board—was a window into the battle we had just left.

I reached out and lay my palm flat on the surface, half-expecting it to pull me in like the giant Shadow—but it was just a smooth, blank slate.

I picked up an eraser and *smack*ed it against the surface once, leaving a white rectangle, before picking up my bag and dashing out of the classroom.

OO9

Kenji dragged his axe along behind him before dropping it as he fell into his pile of abused plushies.

"Weeeelllllllll, weellll, well. *You're* awfully quiet," Miyako noted. "Thought you'd be bouncin' off the walls after finally gettin' your way."

Mm, he murmured—rolling over in his makeshift bed. "Tired."

"Wanna talk about it?"

"I brought the Darkness with me. Everywhere I went, there was Darkness. Too much." He looked over at the bear-like plushie.

Two glassy eyes stared back.

"Too much Darkness. It was hard to see the world."

"Yeah, ya gotta bring a lot with you the first time. It's to tell the world who's boss! But y'know...the more ya go there, the easier it is to take less of the Darkness with you. I mean, how'd ya think I got that snow cone machine?"

"When can I go again?" Kenji quickly sat up, ignoring his sister's explanation.

Miyako didn't answer, and instead she sat down beside him, pushing aside some awkwardly placed plushies. She leaned over and adjusted the new addition to her brother's wardrobe—a patch over his right eye.

"I *said—when* can I *go* again?"

Miyako pocketed a permanent marker, admiring her handiwork—a black *X* on the patch.

"*Miyako!*"

"You're such a freakin' brat, ya know that?" She smacked him on the back of the head.

"Ow!" Kenji rubbed the point of impact and sniffled, tears starting to form.

"You got a chance to leave, you *did,* and now you're whinin' that ya had to come home. Goin' out is *special.* If we could go out whenever we wanted, it wouldn't be *special* anymore—now, *would* it?"

Kenji sniffed, wiping his eye and nose on his sleeve. "I *guess* not..."

"Right. *Now,* lemme give you your most *important* mission yet!" Miyako shifted her weight from her heels to the balls of her feet, standing effortlessly. "Get back to work destroyin' these toys." She gestured. "Some of 'em are *lookin'* at me funny."

OIO

I lay in bed that night, waiting for sleep to wash over me.

Unfortunately, all the thoughts that I had been pushing aside about Chou's disappearance came back in full force.

Especially with all the close calls that Hikari had today.

Judging by how our class reacted when Chou went missing, if someone like Hikari disappeared...it would be held aloft as the school's greatest catastrophe!

Should I have made an effort to keep Chou's disappearance in the limelight?

Why am I the *Grim Reaper* of *magical girls?*

How can I even *think* about sleep when I can still feel the weight of the scythe in my hands?

I slid my right hand out from under the covers and raised it in the air.

Of course, my room is pitch black—my eyes haven't fully adjusted yet, so I can barely make out the shape of my curled hand.

My arm's getting a bit *chilly...*

I shoved it back under the covers, rolling over onto my stomach, arms crossed in a "reverse vampire" position to warm up faster.

Flan Girl...

Are you even *alive?*

Before all of this, I thought you could have been my partner in crime—or justice, *technically*—but with this new information that I'm *apparently Death-incarnate,* I abandoned this line of thinking.

Could I have killed Flan Girl?

I fluffed my pillow and rolled over to my back again.

No—*I* didn't kill her.

Why would I?

What reason would I have had?

I...I must've given Flan Girl *powers,* but it wasn't enough.

She must've had trouble in a battle...couldn't defeat a *monster.*

Which means that I killed her *indirectly,* because I gave this girl powers that weren't *enough...*

That...*somehow* seems worse...

But *maybe* it wasn't a situation like what happened with Chou?

Maybe Flan Girl had her own powers!

And the two of us were just *friends...*

I sat up.

Yeah, I can't sleep.

To make things worse, I have a test tomorrow.

A test that I didn't study for.

At all.

I *was* going to study if I woke up early enough...but didn't anticipate this bout of insomnia.

I turned my bedside light on, kicked the covers off, got up, and went to the kitchen.

If I leave my bedroom door open, that should be enough light to forgo turning any more on, right?

After stubbing my toe on the counter, I flicked on the master switch, immediately cringing from the sudden brightness and placing a hand on the counter to steady myself.

I opened the fridge.

The cavern of flan and pudding greeted me.

Pushing some of it aside, I found that—*yes,* there *was* actual food in there...albeit I *was* getting low on some ingredients...and some foods had probably become science experiments by now due to my *not knowing they were even back there.*

"And of course, I *still* don't know who provides ingredients and prepares most of my meals," I said to no one.

Knock knock.

It was faint, and very quick.

Was that a knock on my door?

Or is my apartment adjusting, and I'm just paranoid because I'm up late?

I inched down the hall, picking up an umbrella from the rack. I undid both deadbolts—if they attack me, I can just transform, right? *Right?*—and swung open the door to face—

No one.

No one was there.

I looked down and saw two bags of groceries.

"Hello?" I called out into the darkness, leaning out my door. "Is anybody there?"

No answer.

Not even the wordless answer of retreating footsteps.

Did they hear me coming...and jump off the balcony?

Can't investigate now—I'd leave the open door exposed in my blind spot, allowing anyone nearby to enter.

I hooked one bag on the umbrella handle and stooped down to pick up the other, slid back into my apartment, and shut the door, triple locking it.

The latch had been undone, so if they had a key they could've *come inside* under the impression that I was *sleeping*—which is *almost* as scary as the idea that monsters are real.

Almost.

Not quite.

Maybe it was just a neighbor. Could we have had an agreement or something that they'd deliver food for me?

I looked at the clock.

But why would they deliver it past *midnight?*

Afterword

I hope you enjoyed reading the first installment of *The Magical Girl in PROXY* as much as I enjoyed creating it! World-building, plotting, writing, and illustrating—all my life, I've loved creating stories with large casts of characters, so *TMGiP* seems like the culmination of all that.

I'm happy that you've chosen this book to join your shelf!

I first came up with the idea for *TMGiP* in December 2015, and really started to flesh things out in January. Originally, I wanted to develop it as a game with my friends, but I proposed the demo for my Honors College capstone project to develop independently.

My thought process for the plot and story went as follows:

- A lazy girl has an app on her phone that allows her to create magical girls and control them. (This is where the "in" part of the title originated—Takako was literally *in* the minds of her proxies!)

- I think Takako was originally going to have her own mascot, but I don't have any drawings of one, so I must have changed my mind early on.

- Takako would have a prophetic dream the night before a battle would take place. Instead of a magazine, *Magical Girl Monthly* was just going to be a notebook—her dream journal—that she used to keep track of events.

- In early January 2016, I had a weird dream involving pudding and flan that made sound effects. It stuck with me for some reason, so I decided to make these desserts the "currency" of the game.

- Around the same time, I came up with the general concept for the main endings (since it was originally going to be a branching narrative with outcomes based on the player's decisions). But I'll talk more about them when we get to the end of the series...

As you can see, my initial idea of Takako differs from how she ended up, and that impacted her interactions with everyone else, as well as the general tone of the story. (The story was also originally going to be in third-person—the change to first-person definitely changed Takako's thought process for a lot of events!)

Though this novel wasn't originally written in Japanese, I took a lot of inspiration from light novels, anime, and manga. I like to describe part of my writing process as "pseudo-translation"—I imagine that what I'm writing is something that already exists, and that I'm part of the translation and localization team. This has helped me with writer's block on numerous occasions, because to some extent I find that writing for pre-existing media is easier at times than writing from scratch—the audience already knows the characters, so minor details can be omitted until I go back into a new draft.

I guess you could say I'm going for *fanime* (fan-made anime) vibes, which is something I dipped my toes into back grade school with other sets of original characters.

I've asked someone how they picture my characters when reading a draft of this novel, and I was really surprised when they said that they imagine everything in live action, as I can't—I can only see the characters and settings as anime, in my art style. Whenever I'm writing, I picture the scene as something out of an anime—with textures and camera angles like *Madoka Magica* or *Monogatari,* or staging like in *Sarazanmai* or *Revolutionary Girl Utena.*

I also want to note that I write my characters' names in family-given name order (last-first), not given-family name order (first-last). I feel like I've been seeing anime subtitles lean towards the latter lately, but I've always had a preference for keeping the last-first order.

The next few pages have some trivia and other points of interest.

Nana's Tongue Twisters

All of Nana's tongue twisters are translated from Japanese—when the first one comes up, Takako asks if they have anything to do with the conversation, but Hotaru says it's just Nana's quirk. However, my choice of tongue twisters actually *do* have a connection to what's happening.

Raw wheat, raw rice, raw eggs

Nama mugi nama gome nama tamago

生麦生米生卵

This is an homage to the first episode of the magical boy anime, *Cute High Earth Defense Club LOVE!* The student council walks by, and one of the main characters says they're daikon radish, egg, and mochi-stuffed tofu—the golden trio of oden ingredients.

So even though Hotaru denies any connection to the previous conversation, Nana really does see Hikari, Yukiko, and Aoi as raw wheat, rice, and eggs...so now the real question is, who's who?

The guest next door is a guest that eats a lot of persimmons

Tonarino kyakuwa yoku kakikuu kyakuda

隣の客はよく柿食う客だ

The "guest" is Tsubasa, and the "persimmons" are her dreams. Nana's trying to say how Tsubasa having strange dreams is just a fact of life, and that she's not trying to be negative by calling them weird.

Nana clarifies that it's "not one of *those* dreams" because a word for "weird" in Japanese has some overlap with "perversion."

Red pajamas, yellow pajamas, brown pajamas

Aka pajama, ki pajama, cha pajama

赤パジャマ黄パジャマ茶パジャマ

This one's obvious—a tongue twister about clothes, said when Nana's retrieving Hotaru's gym clothes.

A snowplow is plowing through the snow

Josetsusha josetsu sagyouchuu

除雪車除雪作業中

Not really obvious that it's a tongue twister in English, but it's obvious why I used it for the scene—Nana and Hotaru are looking at the not-snow.

I laid this bamboo against the bamboo fence because I wanted to lay bamboo against it

Kono takegakini taketatekaketanowa taketatekaketakattakara taketatekaketa

この竹垣に竹立て掛けたのは竹立て掛けたかったから竹立てかけた

I chose this tongue twister because to me, it feels like someone asked you why you did something, and you're saying you did it "just because."

Nana's trying to say that she's neutral about the name "Veggie Girl"—she doesn't really want to transform under that name, but will if necessary. However, she's failing at showing her distaste towards the alias.

Pronouns

In Japanese, there aren't really third-person pronouns that you use to refer to other people (those that *do* exist tend to refer to a boyfriend or girlfriend, romantically). Instead, there are different words that translate to "I," sometimes depending on gender, sometimes on formality.

At one point, I started picturing that Masuyo would use the pronoun *jibun* which translates to "oneself" because they were in the Paranormal Club and just an odd character (*jibun* isn't used often in place of *watashi,* or the more masculine *boku* and *ore*). Because of my pseudo-translation writing process, I decided this would be reflected with "they/them" pronouns.

I also feel that when Nana and Hotaru get competitive, they'd slip in a *boku* or an *ore,* but since they're not using the third-person in this case, it might only come across as bickering.

Glossary of Terms

A couple thousand yen (p.25) — a little over $13 USD as of writing this afterword

Advisor and five members (p.202) — a common requirement for a school club to be made official

Ahoge (p.28) — an exaggerated lock of hair, translates to "idiot hair"

Aiai-gasa (p.215) — love love umbrella; a simple drawing of an umbrella with two names written underneath, similar to writing initials in a heart

Anime (p.20) — Japanese word for all animation

Avant-garde (p.64) — experimental fashion

Bento (p.24) — lunch box

Chuuni (p.140) — short for *chuunibyou;* middle-school second-year syndrome or eighth-grader syndrome; the personality that middle schoolers take on during this transitional period of their lives, often consisting of delusions of secret powers

Clapping hands after a meal (p.26) — part of Japanese table manners, paired with a phrase that translates to "thank you for the meal" or "it was a feast"

Cleaning duty (p.31) — students are given the responsibility to clean the school after hours

Cultural festival (p.216) — a school event where homerooms and clubs run assorted attractions

Fall down seven times—get up eight (p.232) — a Japanese proverb

Flan vs Pudding (p.20) — "flan" (caramel custard) is commonly referred to as *purin* in Japanese (pudding), though on occasion it's called *furan*

Gal (p.55) — the Japanese fashion subculture, *gyaru*

Glomp (p.181) — a tackle-hug

Haute couture (p.64) — high fashion

Kendama (p.135) — a game where you have to land a ball on the handle's three cups and spike; the handle is the *ken* (sword) and the ball is the *dama* (ball)

La Puanteur (p.63) — this does not mean "The Panther" as Aki claimed, and instead it means "The Stench"

Number four is unlucky (p.100) — in Japanese, four can be pronounced as "*yon*" or "*shi*"—the latter is also the word for "death"

Nya (p.55) — meow

Octo-dog (p.64) — a hot dog cut to look like an octopus

Oni (p.74) — an ogre in Japanese folklore, with there being a story about a red *oni* and blue *oni*

Seifuku (p.9) — a school uniform, specifically a sailor uniform

Sports Day (p.121) — the second Monday in October; the *undou-kai* is held annually at schools, and consists of relays and track and field events, among other activities

Seven Mysteries (p.92) — schools and other places often have a list of seven urban legends

Shrimp *tempura* (p.24) — shrimp dipped in batter and deep-fried

Tako (p.181) — Japanese word for octopus

Tamagoyaki (p.24) — Japanese rolled omelette

Tonkatsu (p.24) — deep-fried pork

Uwabaki (p.81) — indoor shoes, often worn at schools

Thank You!

Thank you for reading the first volume, and an extra thanks to those who backed the Kickstarter! Below are the names of those who backed the Super Flan, Flan, and Pudding Cup (with Love) tiers:

J. A. Norman

amphibious-entity

Aaron

Cricket

Ed

Marj

Artemis Cross

Venla Valikainen

Knives

Anita Norman

Sirasit C.

Paul Crispin

Edward Sostre

Cathy